PRETTY REDWING

PRETTY REDWING

Helen Henslee

HOLT, RINEHART AND WINSTON

New York

First published in January 1983 by Holt, Rinehart and Winston,
383 Madison Avenue, New York, New York 10017.
Published simultaneously in Canada by Holt, Rinehart and
Winston of Canada, Limited.

Library of Congress Cataloging in Publication Data
Henslee, Helen.
Pretty Redwing.
I. Title.

| PS3558.E54P7 | 813'.54 | 82-6052 | AACR2 |

ISBN: 0-03-061372-8

FIRST EDITION

Illustrations: Kate Lanxner
Designer: Christine Aulicino
Printed in the United States of America
1 3 5 7 9 10 8 6 4 2

ISBN 0-03-061372-8

To

ELD

Oh, the moon shines tonight on pretty Red Wing,
The breeze is sighing,
The night birds crying,
For afar 'neath his star
Her brave is sleeping
While Red Wing's weeping
Her heart away.

ONE

 THE group of stores and shops familiar to me was not a large one, but I knew them as well as I knew my own home. There was the Piggly-Wiggly, of course; sometimes we went there and sometimes my mother would call them on the phone and order groceries to be delivered.

There was Belk's where she spent hours, seated on a tall stool at the counter looking through the Simplicity Pattern books while I wandered down canyons of printed cotton fabric. She had intense discussions with the saleslady, who wore a smock and had a small scissors on a long ribbon around her neck. My mother made exacting choices of buttons, flat for the back of the dress, round and decorative for the front. I think she sewed as much out of boredom as need.

When we were home again she would unfold the crinkly geometric tissue patterns and—after smoothing out the fabric on the dining-room table—pin the pattern to the cloth, lay the blade of the scissors next to the wood, and then, with a satisfying crunch, crunch sound carefully trim around the maps of tissue. Once used, the patterns were refolded to their original neat dimensions, as though they were secret documents of some planned escape, and returned to the paper envelope with an illustration of the dress-to-be on its cover.

[1]

The words of my childhood were *darts* and *tucks* and *pleats* and *blind-stitch hemming*. The sound was the whirring of the old foot-pedal Singer. Once as a tiny child, having been cautioned a million times never to put a button in my mouth, I put a button in my mouth and swallowed. The excitement that followed was amazing to me. My mother held me upside down and pounded my back. Then she dashed—a stricken look on her face—to the telephone and called the doctor. He suggested that if I was still breathing and not blue in the face the button could be trusted to reappear "out the other end." For some days my mother and I examined the brown pellets of my stool bobbing in the toilet. She poked at them with a straightened wire coat hanger. I found it an infinitely diverting pastime. At last my mother said, "There it is," and gave me a smack indicating her relief.

I liked to go to the shoe repairman's shop. He was missing the tip of his middle finger on the right hand, it having been bitten off by a leather-cutting machine some years back. I enjoyed the game of watching his dexterity while not seeming to stare at his affliction. His daughter was in my grade when I started school, I discovered, and then I was able to invest my visits with another dimension. I could wonder what it must be like at the supper table to watch a grown-up eat with not all his fingers when even the little children had all theirs.

When my mother bought me new shoes it was a treat not only because they would, after they were broken in, become my new friends and constant companions, but also because for each pair I tried on I got to insert my foot into the X-ray machine and watch for the magic needle to point unerringly to my longest skeleton toe and thereby show us all—my mother, the salesman, and then me—just how close that toe came to the inner tip of the shoe.

The local ready-made dress shop was staffed by a group of widows who were of good family and therefore totally untrained for employment of any sort. Some were fairly young, and they dictated the styles that would be available in town. This was in the time just before the brassiere was thought to be a socially necessary garment. Women wore slips and voile dresses in summer, hand-knitted or crocheted sweaters in winter. Bosoms generally seemed to be less perky and more low-hanging then. When we entered the shop in winter a general double-swaying movement greeted us as the widows walked forward to give assistance.

The set in the widows' hair would have been renewed the night before with metal clamps that had clinching centipede feet and reimposed at home on slightly dampened strands the original style, professionally attained at Rose's, where—no oftener than once a week and *never* during a period—sopping-wet hair had been stroked with setting gel, finger-waved into place and baked to perfection under a silver dome.

My nice long curls were usually set in with kid curlers. These were lengths of malleable wire covered with soft leather so that a child could sleep while wearing them. Mine were twisted into place by Sadie before I had my nap so that I would look pretty for the afternoon walk when we joined the other nursemaids and children of the neighborhood. Girls, even while we were still toddlers, were presented to advantage, in our best light, before our male peers, also toddlers.

The other sort of curler was a silver metal tube perforated with rows of holes and possessing a fierce spring grip. They had tiny grommet eyes and an alligator mouth, and always made me feel that a group of baby Louisiana crocodiles was clinging to my head. A person couldn't sleep wearing those, but they were more effective and so were used before state occasions such as a birthday party or Easter Sunday.

The barbershop, with its pole of eddying red, white and blue, was on Main Street. The front of the shop had a plate-glass window and part of the scenery of the downtown area was the semireclined body of whatever man was being groomed. I could never understand how they permitted themselves to be ministered

to in public. The swirling cape, as it was in one matador movement tossed around the collar of a citizen, caught the eye of the
passerby and for the time that it took his steps to cross the front of
the shop he observed, as if attending a drama, the lather stirred by
brush and swept onto the chin of mayor or preacher or bank
president. Then that person, his lower face suddenly an arctic
region, peered out at his comrades on the sidewalk with a slightly
stunned-looking gaze almost as if to say, "Help!" Or if the cus-
tomer was getting a haircut, his head was bent downward to
present the back of his neck to the shears but his eyes were riveted
to the mirror as he enjoyed the narcissistic luxury of a good long
examination of his features . . . not so bad, after all, he *was* a
handsome fellow, quite presentable, yes sirree.

Rose's beauty shop was up a steep flight of stairs in a building housing offices, marginal insurance brokers, not-doing-so-
well real-estate firms, the less popular of the two photographers in
town. We sat and waited on hard chairs or on a secondhand porch
set. On a table covered with one of the shampoo towels were
movie magazines, *True Story* and a snake plant. Adorning the
planter stood a pottery burro, twin baskets slung across his back.
The first time I saw him I leaned over to peer into the baskets to
see what he was carrying. As I exhaled, a swirl of carelessly
deposited cigarette ash flew into my eyes. From then on when I
looked into the basket—to see if, magically, tiny ears of corn or
shocks of wheat had appeared—I held my breath. I held my breath
a lot at Rose's shop. Mostly because of the perm lotion with its
toxic fumes that sucked all wholesome air from the environment
and threatened suffocation.

The permanent-wave machines themselves loomed in
sinister array where Rose could keep a sharp watch on the vic-
tims—swirly-eyed and stiff-necked—who always seemed to be un-
dergoing lobotomy.

Usually I just waited for my mother to have her shampoo
and set but sometimes I had my hair done, too—washed, put in
rollers and dried. Rose's helper, Mattie, was a silent, vacant-faced

girl who drifted into reverie whenever her hands began to massage soap suds into a head of hair. She stood, gripping and probing, and if not roused by a word from Rose, she would press her fingers deeper and deeper into the soft spots of bone until, when I was in her chair, I glanced with alarm up into her face, detected there a manic gleam in her eye and felt a definite longing of the hand musculature to crush whatever skull fell into her grasp.

Mattie also did manicures and put dabs of red on the long nails of plump women who then held up splayed fingers, palm outward, and puffed air on the varnish so that it would dry more quickly and they could return to *Photoplay* and the secrets of William Powell's private life.

WHEN my father got dressed in the morning, if I were awake, I would lie in bed and listen to the sounds of his toilet. When he bathed, he splashed and snorted and I could hear the squeaking of his naked body against the sides and bottom of the tub. It always sounded as though he had drawn an ocean of water, and I could actually hear the waves of it gathering and rolling and breaking against the high porcelain shores of the sea. He would rise from the bath, streams of water cascading and splashing back to the bottom, and begin to groan and dry himself on the towel that he had placed on the radiator to warm. The sounds of a great water beast reverberated against the white tile walls of the room. Eventually he would emerge in an aromatic cloud of talc, a small bald man, and I would peek out the door of my room to see him walk down the hall wearing long cotton drawers with knitted ankles and a scoop-necked, short-sleeved undershirt.

MY mother's private life began in the afternoon. She got dressed for it.

And when Flora got dressed it was like the arrayment of a queen. She bathed in a quieter way than my father, subdued noises

[5]

of the medicine cabinet opening and closing as she took out her lotions and bath salts, bottles clicking on the top of the lavatory.

It was when she came from her bath that the excitement began. She entered the bedroom with me following, her long hair uncombed and her robe loosely closed. From her lingerie drawer she took panties with loose legs trimmed with lace, a brassiere— she was modern—and a slip. These garments were always peach or cream silk. She would slip the step-ins on under her robe, then remove the robe and bend over from the waist to let her heavy breasts hang loose. With little shivers and quivers she would settle them into the bra and, making backward wings of her arms, fasten the hooks. It seemed to me a skill so intricate, to close the hooks without seeing them, that I despaired of ever, in years to come, mastering the procedure. After putting on her slip she would sit at the vanity to do her hair. She wore it in exactly the same style for years—parted in the middle and drawn back over her ears in a bun. When heavy net snoods were stylish she wore one, securing it with huge tortoiseshell hairpins. She walked to her closet and opened the door onto rows and rows of the dresses and shoes and hats waiting for her. She crossed her arms and sighed. I had my own favorites among her dresses, of course, and they were the ones of brightest color with any sort of ruffle or ribbon. I would call them out to her. She had pairs and pairs of shoes—all of which, she said, hurt her feet with their high, aristocratic arches. She was quite vain about her figure, and it *was* lovely—small-waisted, nice hips and buttocks, ravishing legs. Her skin was very pale with sprinkles of red-brown freckles on her arms and hands. Her nails were long and perfectly curved and usually polished in a soft color.

She kept her makeup on the vanity dresser in a blue metal box with a white peony handpainted on top. I would lean over to peer into it when she began to apply rouge and loose pinkish powder to her face. There was always a layer of the soft powder that had flown onto the floor of the box from the puff. I would dip a forefinger into it and rub the silky dust onto my cheeks, arching my neck and looking into the mirror beside her.

Afternoon light came in through the glass curtains on the big windows and the shadows of leaves from the huge pin oaks waved up and down in ever-changing patterns. We could hear birdsong on the soft air and the whoosh of tires as a car passed from time to time on the street below. The slow, then faster, sound of spinning blades and the watermelon smell of cut summer grass told us that Alexander was addressing the endless task of keeping the huge yard clipped and neat.

She would choose her dress, dodge it over her hair, and be off to her bridge game. I would wait for the distant and precise Lily Mae to arrive and earn her after-school money by keeping me out of Sadie's way.

When I had been tiny I slept in this room in a crib with screen sides and a screen top. The top could be left open or could be closed and latched to keep the restless napper from getting out of bed, or to punish the naughty child with imprisonment. Those had all been experiences of mine. I was moved, finally, to a room of my own, but for a long time I would wake up with a start at night to check whether someone had closed a lid over my head.

I return there now, on summer nights, when I am again visited by that unnamed force that brings instant waking from deepest most unconscious sleep, and find that I stand in those lost rooms or, turning between my own sheets, I suddenly catch the feel of covers long since returned to thread.

MY room had a set of maple furniture, a bed with head and foot of turned posts, a dressing table and stool, a chest of drawers. The front windows looked out onto the yard and the street, which was the chief route out of town. The side windows gave a view of the tops of crab-apple trees, in spring a metropolis of pink bloom inhabited by honeybees.

The yard was filled with trees—flowering, evergreen, fruit. Besides the crab-apple there were pear, cherry, red and green apple.

Walnut and pecan. On either side of the broad front walk drooping ornamental umbrella bore pale, pulpy berries. There were dogwood and azalea. Holly and juniper, boxwood and lilac. Wisteria behind the garage. Crepe myrtle and Scotch broom. But the masters of all, towering over the others and over the big stone house itself, were the pin oaks with their long slender leaves that glittered like drops of water in the sun and showed their flat dull undersides when rain was on the way. In autumn the leaves fell and turned crisp and crackling, and because of their thin bodies escaped Alexander's rake again and again, dodging capture and death by flame. Finally, in exasperation, he decided that the most wily escapees would be broom-swept into the flower gardens to act as ground cover for the bulbs.

WHEN Sadie arrived for work in the morning she was given entry into the house by means of a door buzzer that was located beside my parents' bed. My father pushed the button and the lock on the back door was released. Sadie began my father's oatmeal while he was still in bed.

This buzzer and another under the dining-room table were representations to me of the ultimate in twentieth-century technology. The one in the dining room was called a "hostess bell." It was a lump hidden under the oriental rug near my mother's chair. When she wanted Sadie to come in with the roast or to bring my father more coffee, she pressed the buzzer, which then sounded with a snarl in the kitchen. I would crawl under the dining-room table with its thick ankles, carvings like varicosities running up and down its legs, and creep among the broad-bottomed chairs, pushing the mechanism with the heel of my hand until Sadie lost patience with me and came into the room to pull me by the upper arm from under my mahogany roof.

Then I would join her in the kitchen and watch her food preparation.

Sometimes, when neither the farm-girl training of my

mother nor the cabin cookery of Sadie could produce from memory the required recipe, they referred to another source. "Well," my mother would say, "I suppose we'd better look at the *cookbook*." She said it in a certain way. This meant the cookbook that had been left in the house when my father's first wife died. She had been Randolf's mother. Then they would open the flour-dusted, butter-spotted pages of the book bearing on its flyleaf the strong signature "Nettie Cooper Simpson."

The kitchen had a stove with metal legs of a Queen Anne style. There was a sink with long ridged drainboard, a floor of large alternating gray and green tiles and smack in the middle of the room, the kitchen table. The refrigerator, with its burden of spiraling cords on top, was in a special room next to the kitchen. This room was unheated in order to give the laboring refrigerator motor all the help it could get.

All the furniture in the house had been chosen by Randolf's mother. The green plush couch and matching chair that scratched my legs, the ivory-and-blue furniture in the master bedroom, the Mission-style pieces in the sunroom, the rugs, the draperies, the dishes, the colors of the walls, all, all, had been realized from the mind of the first Mrs. Simpson, and in the blunt perception of my father were suited to the use and inhabitance of whomsoever might come to live in the house thereafter. Until they were worn out, used up, and then new ones—new chairs, tables, rugs, wall colors—could be chosen under his guidance.

MY father was a fisherman. Not for profit, of course, but for sport. By the time I was six or seven he was well into his sixties and semiretired from his manufacturing business.

It seemed to me that his greatest joy in life, other than Randolf, was fishing. He liked to hook a trout. And of all trout, the rainbow was his favorite. He had two cronies, younger men, and they both delighted in setting off with him to tramp the mountainsides and foothills of the Blue Ridge Mountains to locate the most obscure creek in all those misty dripping green woods, there to cast, wade and—the two younger men—dip into the moonshine they had bought along the way at some backwoods still.

When he came home, flushed with rare goodwill and general beatitude toward all mankind, my father would lay out the fish for us to admire, offset against their packing of woodland ferns still cool and moist from the riverbank. The fish were silver but with streaks of blush rose and hints of blue. Each tiny scale was itself a rainbow and glimmered with dreamy color or suddenly shot forth a sparkle of truest, pure light.

My father was a fine fisherman and always located for his friends a stream where they enjoyed a good catch. When he returned and announced that they had been "over toward Chesah" or "all the way up past Banner Elk," we knew that he would see himself a hero for days.

The trout were delicious to eat. Sadie created a batter of delicate taste and crunch, dipped the trout, and fried them in country butter. They turned a tawny brown in the pan, their tails curling in the heat, and then we would sit down, my parents, Randolf and I, to a meal of corn bread, trout, tomatoes and cucumbers from the garden, with Sadie's cherry pie for dessert.

The trout's possibility for revenge against the fisherman and his family lay in its spiny web of bones, some cleverly embedded in each tender morsel. There were endless cautions not to swallow these—one ingested rib was guaranteed to bring instant death by piercing the gut of the diner. Just like the hook had pierced the mouth of the trout. Just like the Romans had pierced the side of Jesus.

Fishing was inextricably tangled in my mind with religion. In church I frequently heard the phrase "Thy rod and Thy staff shall comfort me." I knew that the rod meant my father's fishing rod, but I wondered what comfort was offered to the children of nonfishermen. It *was* soothing to watch my father work on his gear at night for a predawn departure.

There was a special cupboard in the house where he kept all his things. He wore a pair of cord pants that he had already had for years even when I was born. He had lace-up boots for bank-fishing when he went for perch or bass, and green gumshoe waders for trout. The creel was wicker. Then there were the rods. There seemed to be scores of them. They were varnished to a high sheen and had rib bands of different colors. There was always a bit of cork on the handle in which to sink the hook for safety's sake. The lures and flies were ravishing creatures, like no insect on earth, more like heavenly embellishments of our crude terra forms.

"Now take this line and walk all the way back toward the end of the yard. Walk slow and I'll tell you when to stop."

In the soft light of a summer evening he would let me help him with his equipment.

I would hold the slender presence, all but invisible in the twilight, and in an agony of responsibility measure careful steps away from him.

"Far enough!"

I jumped at the sound of his voice even though I expected it.

"Stop right there. Now don't let go, but when I start to reel it in, walk toward me. *Not so fast!* You'll tangle it. That's it . . . that's first-rate. Just dandy."

The turning of the reel made a hypnotic sound. In the falling darkness it made me wonder if my father was holding his hands full of crickets and then letting them go, one by one, into the evening air.

Soon we would move indoors and sit in a glow of light at the kitchen table as he rewound and repaired the flies. They were of classical design, proved and repeated; built to pattern. They had names: Brown Bivisible, Near Enough, Red Fox, Pink Lady. Sometimes he created his own on bits of twisted wire. I would watch, my head so close to his hands that his breath ruffled the hair on the top of my head, as though he were breathing life into me, too.

The silk threads that he used were of such seductive, rich colors that they made me dizzy with longing. The lures had gossamer wings, or huge, black sightless eyes, or bodies with soft, enticing gleam. They were housed, each in its own compartment, in a shallow metal box. And each, fixed into its beauty, carried a deadly barbed hook to stab the inner membranes of the mouth that closed around it.

Often, as he worked, he would talk politics to me. He took enormous pleasure of a perverse sort in sitting me down, a child of primary-school age, and explaining to me the exact dimensions of the United States national debt.

"If you had ten thousand men in a room . . . a great, immense room, and each man was counting dollars . . . one-dollar bills, just sitting in that room counting dollars, and each man counted one dollar a second . . . like this"—he paused in his work, moistened his thumb, and took an imaginary dollar from the invisible stack—"each man counted one dollar a second, it would take those ten thousand men ten thousand *years*, counting both night and day, to match the amount of debt that Franklin Roosevelt has brought onto this country. And when you are a woman, a *grown* woman, the money he owes will become a burden that you will have to bear . . . and your children after you. *That* is what the man has done for our country. For *that* we can thank our President. I have no use for the man. No use at-all. For Mr. Franklin *Delano* Roosevelt."

And when he said the name it was with an intonation so venomous, so withering and bitter, I *knew* that all the way up in Washington, D.C.—a place so far away that surely by now it was the dead of night there—I *knew* that the President turned in his sleep and cried out, and from the disturbed depths of his dream drew his hand from under the covers and moved it to shield his heart.

THEY went far back, deep into the wilderness when they fished. They looked for the untouched stream—my father and his friends–the unmarked trail. They listened for a never-before-heard bird-cry. They pulled themselves up slopes clutching the sapling that had split some grandfather rock of the ice age down his brow, they teetered on the edge of cliffs, discovered gorges, left and forgot wives and children, cleaned us out of their minds.

Sometimes they would come upon an old codger, a loner who had built his cabin in misty solitude and lived in isolation, on the chill mountain, in pure nature. Hunting, trapping, fishing, he needed no one and nothing from town or village, required no diversion, no companion, no kin.

My father would return home filled with admiration for that life, and move further into his own private distance. Removing himself from home even while among us.

And when he laid out the fish for our admiration, I began more and more to think about their feelings, the trout's. "Rod and staff" began to sound more like veiled threats than words of succor. I wanted to examine the trout. To poke my finger into their gaping, lipped mouths–to probe the wound, to look for the very atom of flesh that had first felt the sting of the hook. I began to ponder the sudden wonder and despair of the fish whose food had turned to torture.

Their mouths reminded me of a part of myself–not a part that people could see, not a part I talked about or was allowed to touch, but a part that I knew about in secret ways.

What my mother talked of at that time–as he got home later and later, connected with us less and less–was the humor of men gone for a day: how they lost all track of time by the side of a brook. She and the wives of the other two would laugh over the telephone as evening drew on, although since my father was the leader, there was some hint of irritation directed from them toward my mother. She was held just a bit responsible. If she had had more control over *her* husband, then *theirs* would be home earlier. Judson's wife was a peppery, pigeon-breasted redhead who must have had her happiest days as a tomboy, before puberty arrived and caused her chest to betray her. Gabe's wife was a mournful-eyed woman whose German mother-in-law hovered over her home and her marriage like a dark, unmoving cloud.

Maybe my mother never knew why my father needed to leave. Or if she suspected, or knew, in that way we know but don't know everything of importance about those we love, she never released the knowledge to herself.

But leave he did, living among us.

He left his young wife, his child bride, encased in a fine stone house, day after long empty summer day, mother to a spindly little daughter, and stepmother to a quiet, handsome youth.

UPSTAIRS above the two-car garage—like the house, a structure of granite with a green tile roof—there was a rumpus room that had been given over to Randolf. The sloping walls were of wide-plank pine and had a woodsy fragrance. In the center of the room, above which the ceiling rose to a point, stood the green Ping-Pong table that Randolf had built. Against the back wall was his carpentry table with a press for holding the tennis rackets that he restrung, first just for fun, and then, after he had perfected the technique, for money. He had infinite patience and skill, weaving the strips of gut through the dozens of tiny holes drilled in the racket frames. He never snarled the trailing streams of string or mislaid a tool or ran out of supplies in the middle of a job.

He kept his books over the worktable in a wooden cabinet that he had also made. The cabinet had a latched door so that sawdust would not float up and settle on the bindings. The books all looked exciting. They were about Tarzan, and the planet Mars, and many had words such as *sea* or *moon* in the title.

Visiting Randolf was my favorite thing to do, but climbing the stairs frightened me. Because they were built against the outside wall of the garage and open to weather, each stair tread was formed of slats, with space between for water to run off. The first three stairs were easy but after that, as I climbed higher and could see the ground leaving me, floating away under me, I clung to the wall, sliding one shoulder against the sharp stone, at the same time straining with my other arm to reach the handrail.

When I reached the top and stood on the small landing outside the door, I was actually among the highest branches of the little green apple tree. Then I felt like Tarzan. But only for a second. I was desperate to gain entry to the room and stand on a proper floor again.

Thumbtacked to the entry wall of the room were pictures. There were color reproductions of paintings about the American Revolution, photographs of tidy-haired men wearing pleated slacks and playing tennis, blueprints of boats and engineering plans.

Once Randolf had seen on a matchbook cover the pen-and-ink portrait of a pert charmer. Beneath her smile were the words "Draw Me." It was a contest. His version won honorable mention. Every line was just the same. I could look at his enlarged rendering for a long time and detect no difference at all.

Bolted to the picture wall of Randolf's place was a pulley device. It was an exercise machine for strengthening arm muscles. In a pile on the floor beside the machine sat a stack of slotted metal disks that could be added one at a time to the weight supports.

Randolf would stand with his back to the machines, grasp the pulley handles, take a good stance, and with first one hand and then the other lean outward and fling his arm forward as though to punch someone in the jaw. It was glorious to come into the room on a summer afternoon and see him with his shirt sleeves rolled up and his arm muscles rising and bulging, and then to hear the exertion of his breathing. "*Hungh*," a short exhalation with each lunge. He counted the lunges to himself and when he reached a certain number he let me add another disk to the payload. With both hands I would lift the disk and carefully place the slot around the support cord. Then off he went again—lunging, punching, nearly pulling the machine off the wall.

ONE hot, close summer day my mother had no card game. She felt abandoned, she said. All her friends were away on vacations at the beach or in the mountains, and my father had not yet even planned ours.

It was quite possible for him to decide we wouldn't go away at all. He was absolutely free of social constraints of any kind. Seasons meant nothing to him. He vacationed when he was good and ready, if he was good and ready, and gave no thought to whether it was summer or fall or Christmas or spring. I knew that my mother wanted a vacation, not so much because she needed to get away but because she wanted to be able to join in her friends' conversations about theirs and have her own bits to add to the topic.

This day my mother had dressed in a halter top printed with tiny sailboats and semaphore flags. It had a rope tie at the neck and left her upper back entirely uncovered. She had no tan at all, her skin was very milky. She wore blue culottes and, to complete the sailing motif, fabric sandals with rubber soles. She looked quite saucy.

We sat in the backyard, the two of us, in striped canvas sling-chairs, in the shade of the big trees. Sadie brought us lemonade, the ice tinkling against the sides of the moisture-streaked pitcher.

"Randolf," my mother called up toward the rumpus room, "would you like some lemonade?"

His answer came from inside. "I would," he said, "but I can't come down now. I'm in the middle of doing a racket and can't release the pressure on this string."

"We'll bring it up," she said.

She picked up the pitcher and I brought the stacked glasses. I walked on the side next to the wall as we climbed the stairs, pressing my shoulder against her waist.

"Not so close. It's too hot," she said.

The temperature of the attic room was overwhelming when we got there. It was so hot that it seemed to me the top of the Ping-Pong table was curling.

Randolf looked perfectly composed, however. His short hair was crisp. His ice-blue eyes were calm. His shirt sleeves were turned up precisely and neatly to exactly the same height on both arms. There were discreet patches of moisture at each armpit, but there was no hint of anything unseemly or animal about them. His fine hands held the racket gut. His arm muscles rounded, he deftly wove the thin strands and pulled them tight. His tools and unopened packs of coiled string were laid out in order of need to his hand.

She poured his drink and we stood watching him for a while. I grew drowsy and bored. Rivulets of perspiration trickled down the backs of my knees, and I kept turning to wipe them with the hem of my sundress. I gazed at the pictures I had seen hundreds of times before. At the titles of the books. I searched the corners of the room for lost Ping-Pong balls. I walked onto the little porch and gazed into the top of the apple tree. The branches hung heavy with fruit, the leaves slightly dusty and lazy in the still afternoon.

I decided to go back down the stairs and climb the tree to visit my friends the green apples. I ran my hand against the wall's gray stone as I went down. There was little chance I would climb up again alone to rejoin my mother.

I found a cozy crook in the low branches of the tree and there I sat, in a delirium of heat-induced drowse, amid the scent of the polished green globes of fruit. . . the heads of my friends nodded too.

In a bit my mother and Randolf began to play Ping-Pong, the ball in its celluloid perfection, a waxy translucent sphere, bouncing in my mind on the green of the table, over and over again. Once it flew out the door and fell into the tree to join me and the apples, lodging a branch or so above me. I climbed to get it, then strained to meet Randolf's hand as he knelt and stretched his arm between the stair spindles. Our fingers touched, his cool and dry and pleasant, mine sticky and salty.

They played for a while, the sound of their laughter hazy and distant, sweet and young. Then there was a silence while my mother, I suppose, chose a book to borrow from those on his shelf. She came down the stairs, closed and remote, holding a book in her arm, so that it pushed against her breast. I dropped from the tree and we went into the stone house.

I HAD seen Flora paint a picture once. She bought a piece of soft tan cloth that she called "shammy" and paintbrushes and pots of color. First she sketched onto the cloth a mountain, trees, a stream, a deer, a full moon, and standing beside the water gazing at the moon, an Indian brave. He had two feathers tucked into the thong that bound his forehead and a braid of long hair down his back. My mother began to paint the scene with her colors.

She hummed a tune as she worked, and when she put a blush of red on the cheeks of the Indian brave she sang the words to the song. They told of an Indian maid named Red Wing and how the moon shone brightly on her. I was filled with thoughts of how glorious it must be to hold a brush and cause the waters to be blue and the deer brown and the round moon white, a cloud just uncovering it.

Later, I begged her to sing to me again about Red Wing and to lay the shammy cloth out on the hall table where everyone could admire it. She laughed with no mirth and said, "When did you ever hear me sing? I can't sing. That table runner was a mess, and I *despise* this house and all the old furniture in it."

SOMETIMES in the evenings when he had come back from fishing, instead of remaining at home, my father sought the company of men again. If he heard there was to be a country fox hunt that night, he would drive out to listen to the hounds.

The hunt formed at a crossroads filling station. During the hunt a few of the men, the younger ones, would run on foot following the hounds—try to keep up with them over rough terrain, their ankle-high work shoes scrabbling over boulders, crushing brambles, slipping on leaves oily with humus, their faces whipped by brush and thorn, blood roaring, heart pounding—up to the very moment of the kill. Others, my father among them, gathered to sit outside in the crisp night air at the filling station, near where it had been agreed that the hounds would be released and close to the woods where the trail had been laid down.

Rattling, broken-down pickup trucks began to draw up onto the cracked concrete apron of the station. The truck beds were filled with whining, milling foxhounds—soft-eyed, long-eared, very dog-smelling dogs of sweet disposition.

The men stood in groups and talked for a while, some with one shoulder leaning against the unpainted wood of the building or pressed to an old rusting metal sign: RC COLA, BULL DURHAM, BEST WORMING PILLS. A brown bottle wrapped in a wrinkled, twisted paper sack passed from hand to hand. They would take a little cloth bag from an overall pocket, pull open the tie string with their teeth, and tap a row of tobacco onto thin paper, then tongue-moisten and close the edge. The tick of a horny thumbnail sent sulfur up the nose and fire into cupped hands.

They talked quietly with inward smiles as though each knew a marvelous joke and was only holding back from the sharing by great force of will.

At a signal the hounds would be released and begin to circle and snuff until one caught the scent and gave the yelp—a sudden, sharp sound, almost of pain—that the hunt was on.

Then taciturn country faces glowed with rare animation. The runners flung cigarettes to earth and lit out over the plowed ground. Moonlight hit the shapes of hounds and hunters as they made for the woods where the fox sought safety.

The audience left behind sat listening to the concert of bays and cries, telling the translation of them, naming the geography of the trail, waiting for the rise in pitch of the howls that meant the dogs were onto live scent.

"That's my Sal!" A fat farmer suddenly leaned forward, the front legs of his cane-bottomed chair thudding heavily to the concrete. "That's my Sal in the lead! That bastard fox is caught for sure now. Oh, yessir. That fox is dead for sure certain."

"Whoo!" another shouts about his brother. "Whoo! I just *know* ole Malcolm is apantin' an' aheavin' now. Whoo! Tryin' to keep up with them dogs. Whooeee, boy!"

"Lor-*dee*. Just a*lis*ten to them hounds!"

Sometimes the hunt ranged so far that the dog voices began to fade away. Then the men would rush to open their trucks and cars, leap on the running board and reach in to start her up at the same time. They would careen to a spot nearer the creek or over toward Sherrill's Ford or up past Shiloh Baptist Church, the drinking ones tilting rotgut as they drove, the religious fevered by the hunt alone.

Some of the men claimed that the chase was, to the fox, an amusement, an agreeable testing of its evasive skills. Others, champions of the hounds, declared the fox hysterical with fright, driven to the utmost, calling into use its entire store of evasive tactics, eluding the dogs–if it did–only by the intrusion of fate in the guise of a handy briar patch into which the animal darted, or of a hidden ditch into which the lead dog tumbled, or–stretching it–a sudden streak of lightning, producing ozone that momentarily masked the fox's scent.

When at last the exhausted animal was denned, the foot soldiers tormented it from its lair and shot it with dispatch. All that the seated men heard of this was the ringing echo of the rifle reverberating back to them. They kept their patience, though, the sedentary hunters, and eventually, after a number of pursuits, came the moment they desired. Across some valley, over the brook, through the pines, a frenzy of dog sounds, snarls, snuffles, growls, short snapping barks, and then, a filled silence. The dogs had caught the fox in the open and were tearing it to pieces, drinking its exploded, shredded parts.

Who knows what happened after that chase? My father came home and that seemed to be it for him. But there must have been some who heard in the baying voice of the dogs an echo they could not still in their own throats, a call to blood that had never evolved away, and who, when they reached home, mounted another fox hunt. A private one. A chase feverish in intensity, that traveled down dark hollers and damp swamps and wet dewlands till an inner voice bayed, "I've found it, I've found it," and in fantasy they ripped and tore and sank their teeth into blood and brought forth cries from the throat under them, wrung sobs from a stoop-shouldered slattern or a frayed, exhausted wife. Or, rising and jerking alone, met the air, in hoarse, dreamed coupling. "The fox! The fox! *Now* I've killed the fox!"

MY mother delighted in her friends. They were always talking and chatting and gossiping and smoking and sipping Cokes and laughing and exchanging stories and recipes.

All their conversations were like so much formula. Like prewritten dialogue from a play. It was as though each woman had chosen a character and sketched it in. When the other women spotted it, recognized it, they gave her her designation and there-after all conversation was easily fitted to the chosen part. Winnie was oppressed. So when the topic of subjugation came up all looks were directed to Winnie, she was the authority. Leita was a flirt. Trudy was the rich one. My mother, Flora, hated to shop for food and plan menus. They each knew their own part and never tried to steal each other's lines or characterizations.

They played regular bridge and duplicate bridge and went to teas and luncheons and church suppers and fashion shows. They went on shopping trips to the nearest city and to visit the gardens in Charleston in the spring, and once to the World's Fair all the way in New York. They were on the phone to each other and dropping in on each other and in the absence of each other talking about each other. They formed opinions of each other's husbands and children and household help and housekeeping standards. They knew each other's wardrobes and secrets and dreams.

I had great trouble with friendship. I lacked the stamina for it. Either that or I misunderstood the meaning of the word. To me the word implied trust and comfort and a soothing, restful close-ness. A willingness to take time to understand. An agreement to relent in the urgency of one's own demands. But children my own age wore me out. They exhausted me. They were all far more robust than I was. Or they were shifty and sly and hurtful. They plotted. They were capable of schemes. They pinched or bullied or manipulated.

They were unaffected by weather. Heat made me headachy and limp. Cold withered my fingers and toes. Spending the night with a friend, away from my own bed, meant not closing my eyes at all. I became faint and saw black spots in front of my eyes for days afterward.

Other children never suffered hunger the way I did. They

could play hide and seek or skip rope for half a day without pause. If I tried to hold my appetite in check in order to join them, I found myself starved, raving, inside of twenty minutes. I felt in danger of perishing, the lining of my stomach raked and clawed to hemorrhage by my own digestive juices. I turned green and clammy.

When I ate, though, I filled up rapidly and, after several bites, I had to push the plate away, stuffed, sated, bloated.

The appetites of other children astounded me. The energies of other children wilted me. Their capacity for evil terrified me. In fact, any input beyond the range of my own home and family group was close to intolerable to me. I did best in solitude.

At night, when I first went to bed I listened for the trains. The Southern Railway cut straight through town. The Hill, where the black people lived, was across the tracks, along with the commercial laundry and the automobile repair shops. Lining each side of the tracks themselves were the fine old Victorian homes that had been built to border the railroad for a purpose, in the days when there were only one or two trains a day. A man could set his watch by the chugging engine that nosed into the cross-roads, stopping wagons and horses on both sides. He would sit on his broad front porch of a Sunday and nod approval at the iron beast, its power reflecting glory on him and offering proof that the American dream was, indeed, coming true.

Late in the night there was a train that shifted flatcars loaded with lumber onto a siding and picked up closed cars filled with the oak and wrought-iron school desks that were made in town. They were shipped all across the country. I could hear the cars bumping and clanging into each other.

The yardmaster sat up above the tracks in his little house and ordered the cars shuffled like a deck of cards. The engineers lined them up and dealt them onto spur tracks. The brakeman put them into pairs, air brakes howling. The fireman sounded the bell, ringing it over and over again. When the yardmaster won his game (I thought of it as Solitaire or Concentration), the flagman waved the train away. The cars would groan over the hump and be on their way out of town, chugging faster and faster, on to the next junction, the next yardmaster.

Then I would listen to the crickets, the tree frogs, the night birds. I dreamed of trees and fish and animals. I dreamed of swinging too high in my swing and flying out of it high over the lawn. Then of falling, floating, seeing the ground far, far beneath me turning and rising slowly to meet me–a terrible fear in my stomach and spine, night after night. I learned to wake myself from these dreams by a supreme struggle of will. Before I fell to earth. Before I let go the ropes. Before I flew from the branches of the tree.

Once awake, I would read the night sounds of the house: floor creaks, the popping of dry wood, the rustles and turns of other sleepers.

Across the hall there was silence from Randolf's room. He slept discreetly. He didn't give away secrets in the night.

Down the hall my father snored. He was a heavy, loud snorer, his virtuosity truly astounding. He drew in gulps of air, nasal passages and membranes vibrating and rattling in a flurry of activity. Then, after a few steady rumbles, there would be a silence so profound and prolonged that I would startle out of my drowse in fear that he had stopped breathing forever. But then, in hungry, desperate gasps, he rushed to take in air again and regain the balance of oxygen his laboring lungs demanded. There were creaks and sighs and trembles. He would, like a great sailing vessel, make his way, timbers shuddering, across the tossing sea of his sleep. At times I even heard the birds, the gulls, calling from the top of the tall mast as his bronchial branches filled like huge sails, catching the salt breezes, flying forward for a while and then, luffing, he would sigh and tack to find the breeze again, flags fluttering and flapping, his ego, even in sleep, secure on the captain's bridge.

My mother was a restless sleeper, a night wanderer. I would wake sometimes to find her in my room, never looking down at me, but instead standing at the window, her gown floating like mist around her ankles, her hair a dark blur. She would be gazing out the window listening to the mockingbird, her eyes fixed to the glow of the streetlight or caught and held by the silver night-shine of the road out of town.

Once during a heat wave when I tossed all night and appeared for breakfast with lavender smudges under my eyes, my mother said, "Tonight we'll make you a pallet on the floor of your room. It's cooler on the floor than it is in bed. When I was a girl in the country that's what we did on hot nights, my sisters and I."

In the afternoon she had Lily Mae take quilts from the linen closet and pile them on the floor to build a mattress, then tuck a fresh sheet on top. But the late afternoon sun coming through my windows heated up the covers before I ever went to bed. From then on my mother would make the pallet for me herself after dark, and I would lie all night looking up at the window and the limp curtains and the moonlight from an unaccustomed angle. I didn't sleep better, but I rested better. It *was* cooler. After that time I looked forward to hot nights and doing something exactly the way my mother had done it when she was a girl.

I ALWAYS listened to the sounds of the neighborhood as I lay in bed. In the early evening there were the older boys and girls of the block still outdoors and calling to each other or walking by, their steps brushing and crunching on the sidewalk. Later, when it got dark, Miss Chadwick, who lived alone with ten dogs in a house where curtains rotted at the windows, scurried past, all ten dogs romping around her. Several blocks over was the silent, unlit house of the Smithfields. I imagined the stains of blood left on the stairs even after they had been scrubbed. Myron had killed and scalped his mother with a souvenir tomahawk from the Cherokee

Indian reservation. After he killed her he called the police and said that he had done a bad thing but he couldn't remember just what it was.

Out near the country club, Mrs. Garrick bolted her doors every night so that if *her* murderous son escaped from the madhouse, as he had sworn to do, he could not get in to kill her, as he had also sworn to do.

At the country club, the Saturday night party was in full swing. Arriving gentlemen checked with disbelief the initialed scribbles delineating last week's drainage on their private liquor bottles and immediately cut their stares to the black bartender, a much-maligned innocent. Abacus-eyed ladies passed each other in the lounge.

After midnight, some woman's husband would leave the dance floor for the veranda. He would edge over to one of the widows from the dress shop and invite her for a stroll on the golf course. She would laugh and sigh for a minute, then follow him, removing her high-heeled shoes as soon as they were in the dark, dropping them by the pool fence. As they got further from the clubhouse she reached under her skirt and released the hooks of her garter belt. Sliding her fingers under the tops of her stockings, she slithered them off. The man, grinning, put one stocking in his left jacket pocket and one in his right, stirred by the retained heat of her body on the silk. They walked, the widow only slightly conscious of the swinging elastic straps and loosened buckles of the garter belt ever so lightly brushing the down of her thighs. He had a pocket flask. They took a nip. Then, first, they leaned against a tree trunk, he pressing her body with his. A nuzzle, a kiss, and then they sank to the damp green grass.

The next day, Sunday, during games, there would be pauses from time to time as a sap-soaked, lacy pair of step-ins was spied under an azalea bush or half buried, sacrilege, in the sand trap. Each golfer tried, fleetingly, to recall just exactly what he might have done and with whom late the night before.

The scent of flowers rose all over town as the dew of evening settled. In arbors, couples rustled. In the park of topiary shrubbery clipped into fantastical shapes, Tansy's mother wandered and planned her next suicide attempt. In the cemetery, teen-age pairs pressed lips and shivered with delight and excitement at the corruption so near under their feet, so far away in time. And in the Carolina Theater, a Methodist church deacon trolled the ammonia waters of the men's room seeking a towheaded minnow.

IT grew hot again and one night I came downstairs late to ask for a pallet, standing on the bottom step in my gown. In one corner of the living room my mother and Randolf were playing checkers. My father sat across the room, reading the paper aloud to them and ranting about Roosevelt.

"Make me a pallet, please, will you, Mama?" I said.

I waited for her answer. The pool of light from my father's lamp shone on the paramecia and algae that composed the design of the oriental rug. They swam in silent states of agitation.

"Oh, why don't you just go on back to bed," she said. "It's not all that hot tonight."

Randolf made a triple jump.

Flora's eyes and mouth opened wide. She squealed and laughed.

"You don't want to sleep on the floor," she said, studying the board. "There's all kinds of crawling things around in this weather." With a tilt of her head toward her shoulder and a pointed finger, Flora offered Randolf her king. "Earwigs, pinchers," without looking at me. "You don't want bugs in your ears, do you?"

My dreams of trees and animals began to change. More and more I dreamed of myself alone in the big stone house and that there was an intruder seeking entry. Feverishly I darted from room to room searching for a spot invisible from any angle, from any window. As the intruder moved from place to place and peered in, I was desperate to avoid his eyes. If I once saw his face, I knew that he could enter. But if I wasn't forced to look at him, then he would go away. I tried corners, stairs, closets, cupboards, but always, always, there was the shadow of a face. Staring in silently, knowing and finding.

THAT was the summer my father decided that Randolf should do less with the tennis rackets and more with the family business.

"After all," he said, "someday it will be your business. You will find yourself a married man soon and the head of a family."

My mother looked from my father's face to Randolf's.

Randolf began work three days a week in the factory, doing the lowest job, with the understanding that he would be making his way up and getting to know them all.

Sometimes I was permitted to go with him for a morning.

We entered the front office where the secretary-bookkeeper, Miss Elsie, wearing a green eyeshade, sat on a high stool, her firmly corseted buttocks sternly ignoring the delineations of the cane seat. She was a spinster who lived with her weak-minded sister on a farm at the edge of town. Each morning Miss Elsie got up before dawn and, wearing rubber galoshes with the buckles jangling, went out to milk her herd of dairy cows and muck out the barn. Then she heated water, washed and dressed, and put in a full day at the mill. Evenings she hoed her garden, cooked for the next day, and bathed her dotty sister.

My father sat in his back office spinning stories with a salesman or reading and signing letters that Miss Elsie had typed under the ornate letterhead of the firm. My father's desk was a maze of cubbyholes and drawers. There were pen stalks and boxes of gold nibs secured with rubber bands, metal pencils containing cylinders of lead so fragile that if extended too far they snapped under their own slender weight, rolls of postage stamps bearing the likenesses of dreary-faced presidents, a heavy glass dish where a pocked hippopotamus of a sponge lolled in shallow water waiting to lick the mucilage of envelope flaps.

Randolf had gone off to sweep or to bundle looper clips or stack cardboard cones empty of thread. My father took my hand firmly in his and we crossed the catwalk from his office to the mill itself, the ramp bouncing with our steps.

The mill manufactured men's full-fashion hosiery ornamented with clock designs.

We walked high above the big silver dye vats. The sharp chemical smell of the dye as it steeped permeated the mill with a distinctive though not unpleasant odor. The dye men were artists and free spirits who tended to fall prey to strong drink on weekends. Often on Monday a man would have to be bailed out of jail or orders couldn't be met, quotas filled. The mill superintendent would fetch the miscreant from the lockup and deposit him in the office for a stern lecture, not from my father but, far worse, from Miss Elsie. Not a man there had a harder lot in life or could touch the hours she put in of a day, and they knew it. It sobered them for months at a time.

The main body of the mill was a high-roofed twilight place filled with slender-legged knitting machines, their splayed black feet bolted to the floor. They were B-5s from Manchester, England. Men and women who had grown up on the local red clay and had farming bred into their bones stood with awkward plow stance, raw hands guiding the gossamer, insubstantial webs of flying silken thread. The stacked disks of the working parts of the machines whirled in independent directions, hinged digits tapping and touching with furious concentration and geared intelligence. Terrack-a-taca-taca-*touch* as one metal finger flew down to change the pattern.

Bits of lint and fluff lazed through the oily air and the fixers, the men who adjusted the machine parts, wore caps to keep the stuff from their pomaded hair. The women wore V-necked dresses with limp collars that drooped from their slouched shoulders. They had cropped hair that they finger-swept and tucked behind their ears.

He would have to keep close watch in spring, my father told Randolf, dock their pay, threaten to garnishee their wages, or else when the ground softened and the mists began to rise so that you could smell the earth, they would leave to follow the plow and the backside of a mule somewhere, and you couldn't retrieve them for love nor money till harvest time rolled around.

Randolf in his contained and thoughtful way took for his responsibility the creation of new clock designs for the hosiery. He bought stacks of pale green graph paper and sets of pencils with lead of blue and wine and red and composed patterns by blocking in sequences of tiny squares. In the mill he had a quiet authority acceptable to the hands and got as much his way with them as did my father, whose speciality was the direct verbal description straight into a man's face of his numerous and woeful lacks.

IT was a rainy Saturday. Randolf sat at one end of the dining-room table building Mayan temples of clock designs on his graph paper. I sat at the other end with my crayons and a blank tablet. It was bliss to be with him.

"Who did you play with when you were little? On rainy days?"

"Well," said Randolf, "you know how Lily Mae comes to play with you sometimes? I played with a boy named Tom. His mother, Margaret, was in my mother's employ as cook."

Randolf chose his words with deliberation, as though some universal tribunal were tuned to his every utterance. As he opened his mouth to speak, a judge with a long white beard nodded "go" to a scribe who lifted his chisel to cut every syllable onto tablets of graven stone. Randolf never got angry or raised his voice or spoke in hasty temper or couched his words in tones of irony or sarcasm. His sentences moved as white clouds hanging over a fruitful, benign plain. Decorative. No rain, no snow, no searing heat. Ripening, evenly warming, bringing each thought to gentle harvest.

"On rainy days we would play in the hayloft of a barn near the old house, my original home. The house we lived in before this one was built."

I knew the one he meant. The neighborhood had changed considerably and the junkman rented the place now.

"It was still used as a barn then, and there were bales of hay and straw stored up there."

I liked to think of Randolf as a small boy because he still had his mother then. It made me very ill at ease to think of someone's mother dying, although he had been thirteen when it happened and I supposed when you were that old things like death were easier to take. Three years later his father married again, and then my pretty mother became his stepmother.

Not at all like the stepmothers in fairy tales.

"What did you and Tom play?"

"Oh, we showed movies."

"*Movies!?* How could you show movies? In the barn? How could you do that? *Real* movies?"

"They were very real to us."

"Tell me about it."

"First we would arrange the bales of straw into orderly rows of seats. Then we would take a pitchfork and tear down the spider webs off one wall."

I could see the huge enraged spiders, their thick tough webs torn apart, scrabbling for crevices between old timbers, casting over their shoulders incredulous looks as their ancient fortresses were destroyed in one apocalyptic sweep.

"Then we would slide the hayloft door shut till only one shaft of light filtered in. Tom got posters from the display case outside the colored movie house over on The Hill. I'm not sure how he came by them and I didn't want to inquire. Once I asked for them at our movie, and they said, 'Oh, no, we have to send those on ahead to where this picture plays next,' so I didn't inquire how he got them."

"Well, tell me how you got the *movie*, never mind the posters."

Randolf smiled. "Well, the movies *were* the posters."

"What do you mean?"

"When we had the loft all ready, the bales arranged and the door adjusted, then we would take turns choosing a poster and Tom tacked it up on the wall we had cleared. Then we took our seats. That meant the movie had begun."

"You mean you just looked at the poster? It didn't move or anything? You just looked at it?"

Randolf nodded. "Best movies I ever saw."

Light flickered through the spaces between the loft's rough board walls. Flecks of straw and airborne seeds from the hay wafted in the faint illumination. A sepia cowboy rode on his sepia horse, wide chaps flying in the dusty western breeze. His face—the mouth a thin slash—was turned to look behind him at the Indians, their painted thighs gripping pinto ponies, their spears held aloft. Buffalo roamed in the background, covered wagons rounded a bend in the river. Cattle rustlers, branding irons poised, crouched over plump calves. Although the army scout had died, an arrow piercing his chest, he first eluded the brave (who imitated a hoot owl's cry) to summon the cavalry which, even now, smoke puffing from long rifles, thundered through the pass.

Flora came into the dining room and sat down at the middle of the table with her iced tea. "What are you all doing?" she asked.

"Just talking," I said. For a moment I was almost sorry she had joined us. I had never felt that way before.

"Look what I found," she said.

She showed us the gyroscope top that Randolf had given me last year for Christmas.

Randolf chose unusual gifts for me every year. Things that a girl was never given. Playthings a boy far younger than Randolf would have chosen for himself. Things he would have liked to possess at about the time his mother died.

Whenever my top was set in motion the two thin metal circles blurred and spun into a planet poised on slender tiptoe stalk. It whirled along the table surface, or, if set on the lip of a drinking glass, did its dervish dance there, on a crystal cliff, all the while singing its one hypnotic note.

Flora spun the top. It reeled, then righted itself and twirled rapidly. She pursed her lips and gently blew it to the edge of the table surface. It waited. Flora held the tip of her finger just under the table ledge and the top obeyed her, turned, without hesitation, onto her hand. She lifted it—still spinning—and set it on the rim of the cold, ice-filled glass.

"Look at that!" Flora liked the top even more than I did. "Perfect balance." She looked at Randolf. "It doesn't lean too far one way and it doesn't lean too far the other. I admire it. It's daring," she said. "It's daring and it's brave."

TWO

SUNDAY, the day of rest, was an extremely busy and usually unpleasant day. Church bells began to ring early in the morning and tolled over and over, droning on in the same monotoned, ponderous, repetitive way that the preacher was gearing up to imitate.

I got up and then, in order to be sent off to Sunday school on time, I had to rush through the breakfast of pancakes and bacon over which the adults lingered. Drifts of the bacon smoke lazed in clouds and pockets, rising up the stairs and mingling with the dust motes glinting in the sunlight streaming through the windows. The very air was different on Sundays. The collected staleness of the week assembled and crowded into lungs and spirits. Sluggish roils of boredom inhabited the soul. The most fascinating pursuits of the week turned to sediment, sludge, leavings. Even if you had just come in from a trip halfway around the world and had no idea of month or date, I was convinced you could tell for sure whether or not it was a Sunday. On that day, air and time stood still.

Sunday school was held in the morning before regular church services. The classroom had a linoleum floor and a dank mildew smell of subterranean origin. Like all other rooms that nestle deep under the soaring structures of steeples and gothic ceilings, it seemed to carry the smell of mortality. Of the return to earth. They remind that it's all very well to sing of Easter and pray to the Redeemer for the wings of angels and eternal life, but remember, O Man, what comes first.

Sunday school was a religious experience for me, my soul nourished and fed, but not in the way the church fathers must have hoped. It was because of the illustrated papers we were given. They were four pages, slick and glossy, the smell of ink dark and rich. They smelled as if they had been brewed rather than printed. The flowing purple robes of Jesus were grape-ade. The tawny desert sand was butterscotch. I savored them deep in my throat.

In fact, the Bible itself seemed to dwell heavily on the topic of food. The Israelites were always devouring figs and honey, apples and dates, lambs or kids, drafts of wine. It made me think of the country club or the Rotary. Loaves and fishes. Grapes. Goblets, pitchers, skins of wine. They never had to eat things like okra or stewed tomatoes or snap beans. I wondered where in all that sand they could cultivate their crops. The papers portrayed an endless desert, a palm tree here and there, a few clay houses with slightly raised dome roofs, and figures clad in wind-tossed robes. A camel would be tethered nearby in case anyone had to get over to the Chaldeans to make a covenant.

The biblical custom of anointing with oil bothered me terribly. It seemed to be a ritual of the time to carry a little jug of olive oil and upon meeting, friends, as a courtesy and mark of respect, would drizzle some over each other. It tortured me to imagine what that must be like in such a burning hot land with no bath water to speak of. I saw Jesus and his friends as constantly sticky, covered with a sheen of grease and then a layer of grainy particles. Goodness only knows what transpired during fierce sandstorms. Their robes *had* to be a sight, I thought, dotted with spots and smears of oil. It was doubtless this which attracted the swarms of devastating locusts every seven years.

Another courtesy was foot washing. The weary traveler

would no sooner stagger into town than some good Christian would pounce on him, remove his sandals (a terrible adjustment to make, the idea of a man wearing sandals) and plunge his dusty feet into a bowl of water straight from the Nile. Once when someone washed the feet of Jesus and the lady of the house had run out of towels, she dried His feet with her hair. How did she get the idea to do that? I simply could not imagine any of the women I knew coming up with such a deed. Trudy? Maybe Leita, the flirt. What possible response could Jesus make to such an assaulting social performance? There were no surviving prayers that I knew of on the topic. All the preachers liked the story, though, and centuries later paused during the reading of the text to direct a gaze at some flushed matron in a flower-bedecked hat with veil.

THE house no sooner partially cleared of bacon smoke than it filled up again with the smell of *well-done* roast beef. Brown. Brown from top to bottom, from fat crust to inner bone. With dark brown gravy and mashed potatoes and green beans cooked to stupefaction in fatback. My mother did the Sunday cooking herself. Chopped iceberg lettuce with mayonnaise. Sometimes a canned pear cupped this dressing. Hot biscuits, they were good. Iced tea, that was good. Apple pie that Sadie had made the day before.

The meal over, Randolf went to play tennis. My parents and I climbed into the car.

The ride to my grandparents' house was eighteen miles of distilled nausea. Gray fumes from my father's Lucky Strikes filled the car, closed so that my mother's hair wouldn't muss. The backs of my thighs chafed from the scratchy seat. The conversation between them was dour and bleak—about the sermon, the roast beef, the weather.

We got to my mother's childhood home by driving down a rutted washboard of a road. The road, cut down into the earth, curved and slanted in its attempts to achieve control over the persistent drainage problems posed by the seizing, clasping red clay. The clay was never bested. Halfway down the road a board bridge crossed the gulley which in spring carried rust-colored runoff. Trees and brambles made hasty grabs for the sides of the car, and the weeds that grew in the center of the tire tracks went ping, ping, thump as they hit the underbelly.

The cleared ground to one side of the road grew cotton, the other corn. Closer to the house was Flora's mother's vegetable garden. Daffodils marked the borders in April and marigolds all summer.

The house was two stories tall and three rooms wide in front, with the kitchen and dining room tacked on at right angles to the rear. A corrugated tin-roofed porch spread from one side to the other, supported under its corners by stacked stones. Tall oaks spilled capped acorns onto the tufts of wispy grass below.

The side yard of the house was the working area where the mule was watered, chickens scratched, and the hounds dozed. The bare dirt yard was swept every morning by one of the girls who still lived at home. The area was considered almost part of the house. The well was located here, surrounded by a shallow cement floor and covered with a little pitched roof. The barn, pigpens, an abandoned buggy and the outhouse were all some distance away.

Inside the front room a wood stove burned pine logs most of the year and harder woods in harsh weather. During all seasons the room retained the fragrant smoke of winter.

On a small table covered every week with a fresh white cloth sat a Philco radio connected to two dry-cell batteries each the size of a quart bottle. When the radio was turned on either hillbilly music or hymns played.

The bedrooms led one into the other with no hallways between. The covers were quilts made of sewing scraps—bits and pieces leftover from family garments—and stuffed with cotton grown on the farm. My mother would sometimes point to a patch of quilt and tell me that the print had been from a dress made new just for her. Not a hand-me-down.

My grandmother Minnie's kitchen smelled of flour-powdered yeast bread with a hint of carmelized sweet-potato sap. She always gave me a big slice of bread with hunks of home-churned butter on it and shook her head over my skin and bones. "Nothing but skin and bones. And all that long, hot hair."

Minnie was a short, redhaired, sharp-eyed woman. Her gaze, even from behind gold-rimmed glasses, went to the gut, found the weakness, and dealt with it. She was bowlegged from ten pregnancies and deliveries. As each baby was carried in the womb the family laundry basket that was hefted along with it grew heavier. Minnie wore an iron-strong corset to support a back given out.

Mornings, my grandfather Rawlings would bring Burt into the farmyard and there would be a great deal of resolution, flurry and purpose about him as he adjusted the traces and gave Burt a pep talk about the day's work ahead. Man and mule would then set out for the fields, but it wouldn't be long before the call would come from a distance: "Whooo, Minnie. Whooo, Min!"

The crows rising from the field with his voice marked the spot. Minnie would walk out, carrying along a beaded mason jar of well water, and help Rawlings solve whatever dilemma had brought his work to a halt.

Rawlings was a totally ineffectual, completely charming man. His merry blue eyes made his face trustworthy and devilish at the same time. Women adored him. His eight daughters clustered around him whenever they were home. Minnie had spent a good portion of her life following his gaze as it leapt and played from one bosom in the country choir to the next, from the organist to the preacher's wife, from the confessing sinner to the young angel being confirmed. There was not one woman in the world who ever had enough of him.

I thought he was as much my father's opposite as a man

could be. My father was well-to-do, Rawlings could barely make a living. My father was a Republican, Rawlings thought Roosevelt was God on earth. My father hardly ever touched me, Rawlings grabbed me and tossed me in the air and called me his girl and implored me to give him kisses whenever we visited. "Give me some sugar," he would fairly wail. "Come on now, give me some sugar. Give your granddaddy a kiss and a hug."

As far as I could tell the two men were alike in only one way. Age. Flora had married a man the exact same age, to the very day, of her own father.

ANOTHER baby turned red in the face. Its cheeks quivered and swelled in infant apoplexy. So far it hadn't made a sound.

My father looked down at me. "Now," he said.

As we stepped off the porch he continued our conversation.

"At five in the morning he would reach his hand out from under the covers and take a broom that he kept next to the bed and poke at the ceiling. That meant I was to get up and light the fire in the kitchen stove and in their bedroom."

"And you slept upstairs?"

"It wasn't a real upstairs. More an attic. Up under the eaves. Cold as the dickens. Bitter. And in summer hot as the hinges of Hades."

"And you had to get up first?"

"Well, he was a merchant prince, my father, your grand-father on my side. That's how he saw himself"—a dry laugh—"as a merchant prince. Stop a minute. You see that little pile of leaves over there? Under that sapling? Brush away those leaves. Be real careful."

I knelt and picked the leaves away one at a time. When I had removed them all a plant with one big overhanging striped leaf was exposed.

"Now lift that leaf."

I did. Inside a tiny cup stood a slender stalk.

"That's a jack-in-the-pulpit," said my father. "The Indians used to eat the roots. Gives a better sermon than our preacher, doesn't he? Lasts longer, but it's quieter."

I looked up at his face. He was smiling. This was one of his jokes. I smiled, too.

We continued our walk. When we walked on dry leaves they crunched. When we moved on pine needles all was quiet. Both were nice.

"And he was the one who fought in the War Between the States? Your father?"

He nodded. "The battles of Gettysburg, the Wilderness, and Spotsylvania."

The names sounded biblical to me. I knew by then in time men wore uniforms but I saw them in robes anyhow. On a desert. In chariots.

"He was a young man then, not yet married to my mother. The worst fighting he saw his first day in battle was among eight Confederates. They were smashing at each other with their rifle butts. Each man wanted possession of a captured Union flag." He paused. "You know, your worst enemies are not always on the other side." He got quiet for a time and seemed to lose his train of thought.

"And then what happened?" I asked.

"Well," he said, "the fighting went on and his regiment faced cannon battery and he saw men torn asunder, torn apart, and the threads of their flesh thrown into the limbs of trees."

I looked at the pines and maples and thought of strings of blood clinging, forming, dripping, drop by drop, onto the moist ground.

"Then they retreated down the swollen Rappahannock. At Spotsylvania he was captured. By drunk Yankees. They almost shot him, but an officer appeared just in time to control the enlisted men. And then he was shipped by train to an army prison in Elmira, up in New York State. Nearly died. Starvation. Destitution. War is a bad thing. A bad thing. And I hope to God that pompous maniac Roosevelt doesn't get us into one."

When he mentioned Roosevelt I knew he would be stopping soon for a smoke. We came to the brook and he halted. He tapped his pack of Luckies and one answered, poking its head out. He withdrew it and bent over to tamp it on a flat boulder.

Tamp, tamp, look at the end. Tamp. Tamp, tamp, tamp. Look. He always did it in exactly the same rhythm. When he was satisfied that the tobacco was as tightly packed as it could be, he lit the cigarette and inhaled deeply. "Ahhhh," he said, calmed. Then he brushed the particles of tobacco off the boulder just as though it were the end table beside the couch at home.

We stood on the boulder for a while looking into the water for baby fish. He could spot them in a minute, but they darted and swam so fast they were gone before my eye could follow his pointing finger.

I had seen old-fashioned photographs of his parents. The father was a tired-eyed man with white hair and a dark mustache. The opening of his jacket seemed to curl out too far. Leaving too much of his chest exposed. He looked injured, exhausted.

The mother had a face like a hatchet. A look from her could split you in half. Like dry kindling. I was relieved she was dead and gone.

"And you worked in the store even when you were a little boy?"

He nodded. "Swept up, shoveled snow. Took the mice out of the traps. Folded the dust covers. Sold cloth. You know how they measured cloth back then?" He bent his right arm and stretched it out as far as it would reach. The left hand flipped an imaginary bolt of cloth and guided the goods through his fingers. "Like that. That was a yard of cloth. From the end of your nose to the end of your arm. Tricky shopkeepers tried to hire boys with a short reach. Ha!" A smile and a shake of his head. "Sold high-button shoes. Sacks of grain. Everything. All in one store."

"And your father was the owner?"

He nodded again. "My father and a partner. It was a partnership. The other man had no son. My father and I planned to buy him out. Over time. Work hard, save, and buy him out. Then we would be partners, my father and I. But he was crooked. He was a crooked man. He took all the profits out of the savings bank and disappeared. Off the face of the earth. Just disappeared. Broke my father's heart."

He looked down at me. "That's when I decided that I would *never* have a business partner other than my own sons. Never put my trust in any man not my own flesh and blood."

"And now you're bringing Randolf into the business," I said.

He nodded slowly, still looking at me. "And when I married your mother I hoped for more boys. More sons."

A bee hurtled past my ear, startling me, and flew away with my first response to what he had said. As I collected my thoughts again, I supposed that it seemed quite reasonable of him to want sons. I knew who ran the world.

"What happened to the family after the crooked man stole all the money?"

"My father began to farm the acres he had, and I came into town and got a job at the lumber mill. Five dollars a week. That was my wages. Five dollars a week and I sent home four a month and paid my room and board and put savings aside, too. Every week. And after a while I met Randolf's mother-to-be and we got married."

"What was she like? Randolf's mother?"

"Proud," he said. "Proud and haughty."

"I thought those were not nice things. That we're not allowed to be proud and stuck-up."

"Some people are born that way and they don't even know it. It's just the way they are. They can't even tell. She was that way. Proud."

"Was she pretty?"

"Oh, yes. She was pretty."

"As pretty as my mother?"

"Well, different. A different kind of pretty."

Randolf was an only child, and he didn't have any aunts and uncles or cousins that I knew about. I thought of my mother's seven sisters and her two brothers back at the house talking and laughing and telling tales on each other. And Rawlings and Minnie listening and smiling. The numbers of babies stumbling around and the husbands and wives all lined up on the rush-bottomed chairs, the hubbub and noise of it all. My father told me his family had been very quiet, with him an only child, like Randolf. His parents thought chatter meant you had an empty mind. They never talked about how they felt about each other or mentioned any emotions at all. His mother thought that bespoke weakness, my father said.

"Was Randolf's mother an only child?"

My father looked at me thoughtfully. "Let's cross the branch. See how the stones make a path across? Somebody put them there, in place like that. That's a poor man's bridge, stepping stones. I'll go first and show you how." He stepped across easily.

The stones had been spaced for adult steps so I had to jump to make it from one stone to the other. He held out his hand to me and I leapt to shore.

"Nettie had a brother, Frederick. He would have been Randolf's uncle. He was my friend. That's how I got to meet Nettie. Through him."

"What happened? Did he die, too?"

"Well," said my father, "Frederick had a jealous wife. He worked for his father, they had a barrel factory, and he was office manager. And every day, at a different time each day, his wife, Martha, came to the factory. Walked over from the house to make sure he was at his job, where he was supposed to be. Not out somewhere with another woman. Naturally, this embarrassed

Frederick. Made him the butt of jokes and so on with the workers there. And he loved her. He never got angry with her or told her to stop or whatever. Never let her know how they made fun of him. Furthest he ever went was to get a telephone put into the house. Telephones were new then. Nobody much had one. Who invented the telephone?"

"Alexander Graham Bell."

He nodded. "Right. So Martha would ring him up on the telephone. Had to crank them up in those days. And he would answer and say he was right there, in the office, she shouldn't worry. But the distortion on the line was so bad she didn't believe it was him. Couldn't recognize his voice. So she would come over anyway. To the office. And then she would say, 'You were out and had somebody else answer. You played a trick on me.' And things like that."

He went through the cigarette-lighting ritual again.

"The only time she was happy, Martha, easy in her mind, was when he was with her. When I was courting Nettie I would go over in the evenings to the big house, they all lived in with the old man, Nettie and Frederick's father, Mr. Cooper, I would go over in the evenings and we would sit in the parlor, the four of us. Talk, look at pictures in the stereopticon—you know what that is? It's what we had before moving pictures came about. And we would sing. Freddy had a good voice. Tenor. Fine voice. He and the girls would sing and I would whistle."

He did some of his fancy whistles for me. Trills and birdcalls and chirps.

"So he would sing, and that's when Martha was easy in her mind. When he was with her and singing love songs."

"So what happened?"

"Nettie and I got married. We had the wedding in the church and then all went back, all the wedding party, to the big house for a meal. Sat at tables in the dining room and in the parlor and the front hall. Crowd of people. All over the place. Well,

Martha got it into her head that one of the bridesmaids was making up to Freddy. Said she was fluttering her eyelashes at him and smiling over her shoulder and all that sort of thing. The girl was my cousin. Nettie hadn't even wanted her in the wedding, said she was too 'country.' But since I didn't have a sister, she had to have the cousin. Or so my mother said. Well, Martha got angry. Furious. Out of control. Began to rip at the girl's dress, grab at her throat. Upset tables. Nobody could calm her. Certainly not Freddy. Whole place was in an uproar. Spoiled things for Nettie. She was so upset she couldn't travel. Had to delay the wedding trip."

I gently touched his arm after a while so that he would remember to start talking again.

"After a day or two . . ." He cleared his throat. "After a day or two, Martha seemed all right. Nettie and I left on the train for Niagara Falls. A week passed. Then Martha appeared at the office again. Just the way she always had. Freddy was very patient, kind to her. Like always.

"When she left, she said it was so nice and sunny out that she would take a shortcut through the work yard and go shopping. Freddy thought that sounded encouraging. She insisted that he not walk with her, that she had interrupted him enough already. Freddy resumed his work, but after a few minutes he heard a strange sound from the yard. From the back, where they had the truss hoops and stave machines. He went to the window and saw some of the men pointing up at his office. He kept hearing a sound like bells ringing. Freddy went down to the yard. When he walked around the corner of the building he saw Martha and one of the workers with their arms around each other, imprisoned, caught fast by hoops that had fallen from a broken wall peg above them. That tumbled and slipped over their heads as they stood in an embrace. And other hoops still fell, bounced and rolled with a lovely sweet sound all around the yard."

He unlatched the gate from the pasture to the dirt road. We

went through and he turned to secure it again. Then we walked down the road toward the farmhouse.

"From that day on, Martha was completely mad. Her father had to take her off to the asylum. She got herself into some kind of Roman nun outfit for the trip. She lived there for years. Died there."

"What happened to Freddy?"

"Freddy put a rope around his throat. Hung himself. Put a rope around that fine, useless voice."

"War is bad and jealousy is bad," I clipped out. I always rushed to deliver the "moral precepts" that I had drawn from his talk. That was our understanding. To end our walks and discussions with a summing up.

"Things are not always what they seem," he said. "More toward that, I think. Of course, sometimes things are exactly what they seem. That's the trick, all right. To know which is which."

Later, as we got back into the car for the drive home, I thought about the early dinner of cold leftovers that we would have. Then, before bed, I would listen to my favorite radio programs.

Minnie drew my mother around toward the rear of the car as my father slid into the driver's seat.

"Remember what you have," she said.

I looked into my mother's hands to see what Minnie had given her—a jar of sauerkraut or some damson preserves. But Flora's hands were empty.

T HERE had been gifts. A beaded evening bag, a comb and brush set. There had been evening drives to resort towns to dine in the hushed carpeted spaces of fine hotels. The road climbed the sides of mountains. His automobile had white sidewall tires and a belted luggage compartment that was shaped like a steamer trunk.

The headlights cast their glow into space each time they drove around a curve, and only when she was certain it was too late did the lights find the road ahead and spill over to illuminate the bluff the car hugged as well. The ride thrilled her. She hoped they would crash—fly out into the fog and plunge straight downward for miles through soft wet air. It kept her from thinking about his question and the answer she knew she would give.

When the headlights shone over the void, the drop, it thrilled her the same way the idea of the man thrilled her. The man himself was direct, blunt. When he was charming it was summoned charm. He was not engaging by nature. There was too much of the serious-eyed child in him; the echo of that harrowing gaze children have when their lives have been given over too early to adult concerns. A ghost followed him. She only hoped it was not the ghost of the first wife. That would be difficult. That would make it hard.

The evergreens and laurel along the way had been polished by mountain rain and gleamed with a special luster near the resort area. Money actually seemed to seep into the soil around property of the rich whose gloved hands never touched the earth but whose persuasions were not easily denied, even by nature. In the hotels the flatware that idled on the heavy linen tablecloths was the size of weapons. The water goblets were tankards, the plates platters. The rooms were cavernous, the fireplaces immense structures of native stone alien to any stone she might have recognized as having glanced and sparked under the blade of a plow.

The softly gowned women knew where to place their gloves, their clutch purses, their wraps so as not to interfere with the waiter's hand, the steps of passersby. The accepting of the menu alone became a work of art. The slim hand cast out, palm upward, fingers gently curved inward, wrist slightly bent.

She learned. Observed the placing of a jewel here, the tilt of a hat there, the draping of a shawl, the sidelong glance, the staircase glide, the bracelet to enhance a wrist bone, the shoestrap to embrace an ankle. Pauses, hesitations in speech and then, unexpectedly, a delighted and hearty laugh.

It was an art form no woman ever had to directly teach another. Each artifice inspired another. Each male response rewarded the art. Once learned, perfected, it seemed a pity not to need it again after marriage.

WHEN he picked up his newspaper and began to wait for her to bear a son, when the dining out no longer occurred and the evenings grew long, when her energies threatened to explode her, when having possessions was no longer enough to fill her thoughts, she looked, just looked, at the boy.

He had definite lines. His sandy hair outlined his face, his profile was sharp, his body clearly drawn. He could be recognized, distinguished from a great distance with stunning clarity. She could see him coming for miles. His self was etched on the air that surrounded him.

After the wedding trip the man brought her to the stone house. The boy was in high school. Before the marriage she had not thought much about the reality of their day-to-day living: That there would be two men in the house. That they would compose a family of three people. That every night when the husband and wife lay in bed, the boy would be breathing, in rest, just down the hall. That the touches of man and wife would take place as a third person lay within hearing.

She had thought that she could take her time, that if she didn't like what he wanted to do she could withdraw, be coy, cry a bit, flounce from the room. She found herself instead a quiet prisoner.

Sometimes she thought her loneliness would surely kill her. Her vision of marriage had been a closed society of two people who give aid and comfort to each other against the outside world, forever and ever. She had thought in terms of evenings thick with camaraderie and mutual dreams of mutual goals, undefined in her mind but real nonetheless. It wasn't that way at all. He simply wanted to continue some private vision of a dynasty he had fixed on.

She would try tuning the radio to music, but that broke her heart, made the oneness terribly perceived, achingly realized.

There was a certain light that settled in at about six in the evening that slowed time, encased her in her separate being. She had hoped for a resonating reunion at the end of every day, a coming together of twin spirits who had been unwillingly parted in the workaday demands of the universe. She saw it not so much as the locking of bodies, although that was surely part of it, as the meeting of souls who, together, could hold off the void.

Simple things such as the sounding of a car horn could pierce her heart with its meaning of lost promise. The twitter of a bird, the falling of a leaf, demolished her, left her sobbing. A foolish crooner could casually sound a note that would leave her wrecked without hope of salvage, as though she had just been informed of some monstrous loss, some tragedy of universal disorder.

One morning she walked to the door of his closet. It had a full-length mirror. She glanced at herself. Then she opened the door and left it as far toward the wall as it would go so there was no chance of her seeing herself again. She looked at his things hanging there. The suits in sober colors. The wool vest fronts with silk belted backs. The hatboxes with swooping lids. The rows of black leather shoes. The heavy silk robe. He had and wore no informal clothes. He always dressed in a suit with a white shirt and a conservative tie. She felt no impulse to wrap her naked body in any of his things.

She went to his chest of drawers and opened the topmost row: piles of handkerchiefs, boxes of studs and cuff links in one, mounds of socks from his own mill in the other, some boxes of new socks covered with crisp paper and tied with red twine.

His shirts were laid on top of each other in such a way as to show their decapitated necks, bare of collars. He still wore collarless shirts although they had gone out of style. His were in good condition so he stubbornly continued to wear them. Piles of starched collars lay in the next drawer with the wooden tabs that secured them to the neckpieces.

In the bottom drawer were the old sweaters and shirts that he could dress in with impunity when he went fishing.

She had seen all his things before. She wasn't quite sure what she was doing, but she continued to open drawers and push garments aside and generally peer around.

On top of his dresser she spotted his pocket watch. He was particularly fond of it and carried it every day except when he went fishing. She couldn't imagine why he had left it behind today. She wondered if it was broken. She picked it up.

The watch had a white face and handsome black hands and numerals. Each minute demarcation was strongly defined, sharp and firm. The back of the case was silver-etched with vertical lines. She gave the stem a turn. It was almost fully wound. He must have wound it and put it down again.

She moved to replace the watch on the dresser tray but continued to hold it instead. She lowered it and pressed it to her mons. She could feel the tick tick clearly.

FLORA dressed in her maternity clothes for the first time and went downstairs to find the boy.

AT first she felt that he owed her something because of those nights with the man. But then, when she couldn't get behind his eyes, she became enraptured by the game, the challenge to break through, to make him show something, reveal something.

It crossed her mind during the first months that maybe he was too young. There was three years' difference in their ages. Maybe she had grown up faster because of her hard life.

When she had been his age Minnie had been pressing her to go for nurse's training. That had been Minnie's scheme for getting the girls away from the poverty of the farm. The two boys would take the land, but all eight girls would go for nurses. Several of Flora's older sisters were already working in the county hospital. Flora had had mixed feelings about it all. Then at the end of high school there had been a classmate, Frank, whose family were well-to-do farmers, who took an interest in her. He admired her high cheekbones and puffy underlip, compared her to her sisters, and told her she was "the pick of the litter." But one night she lifted her lips to his for a kiss and found, where his mouth should have been, a hot dark hole. It repelled her. She tried the kiss on one other occasion with the same result and then she knew she would go for a nurse.

So the boy was not too young. Boys that age were thinking

of having women. Of holding them and running their hands over them and doing things to them. It was not that he was too young.

The boy appeared interested in what she said—polite, comradely though cool. He took great pains to make certain that she understood everything he said but nothing that he thought or felt. He drove her wild. She began to use the tricks, the artifices that she had collected and proven in other company. He didn't seem to recognize the game. She found herself becoming more and more her true self with him; still there was no sign of his opening up, not a chink that she could slip through. There was no way for her to crouch silently beside a hole chopped in the ice and await his ego coming up for air and then, wrapped in the furs of her vanity, pierce him with her spear, watch his blood foam and bubble, watch him sink below the surface feebly moving his limbs, imploring her with his numbing eyes.

It went on and on. She made friends, went places with them, created a life around the empty space that should have been a marriage, but always she came back to thoughts of the boy. And her struggle to get him in some way. It became her work, her job, her vocation. It was what she did.

THE Examiners wore dark suits and tall black hats. They probably came only a few times a year, although there was a platform of benches for them against one wall, a threatening reminder even when empty. The Examiners had beards and mean slit eyes and thin knowing smiles.

They picked her out as one the minute they entered the room.

For the first day or so they only listened to the lessons. The schoolroom seemed to be an old-fashioned one, Victorian or something, but since she didn't know much history she didn't bother to work out the details. The children she thought of as orphans, with no one to turn to for help. The girls wore long dresses, the boys had loose shirts and high-top shoes. They had slates instead of paper and pencils.

There were two regular teachers. A man and a disdainful older woman.

The children arrived one morning to find a makeshift sort of curtain or drape hanging behind the teacher's desk. The Examiners, from their bench, could see both behind the curtain and into the classroom. This morning they had indescribable smiles on their cold faces. And then she knew.

The woman teacher called her to the front of the room. All

eyes were on her. "Go behind the curtain, Flora," she said.

Flora tried to protest, began to shake her head, but the teacher took her by the upper arm and shoved her behind the drape.

"Do as you are told or we will take down the curtain and let your classmates see."

One of the Examiners stood up and left the row of benches. He walked toward her as she stood, body paralyzed, shaking her head. He pushed her to the floor, where there was a thin pallet. He began to remove her clothes. The man teacher came to help. They began to rub her body, thighs, between her legs. She grew wet. The Examiners began to breathe more heavily, audibly, and in front of the curtain the children were forced to continue their lessons, spelling out words, doing sums, the woman teacher drilling them, but from time to time stepping back to peer behind the curtain and smile with icy clarity at the scene taking place there.

Flora began to moan, to feel a strange will for the tormentors to continue their evil touches.

"I knew she was one," they murmured to each other.

From time to time an Examiner not directly involved in the proceedings would step down from the raised bench to peer more closely at her private parts.

"Tomorrow we will do this again," they said, even as they continued what they were doing at the moment. "We've found you and now we will do this to you again and again and again."

She was in a state of unendurable sensuality and shame. Humiliated. Sobbing and longing. They were right. She was one. She was.

Flora cried out. It was the first time she had ever come. It was early morning and the man was looking at her with a pleased expression as they lay in the room with ivory-and-blue furniture. She was quite far along in her pregnancy, her belly a mound under the sheet. He sank back to the pillow in spent stupor and groggy pride.

WHILE she was pregnant she and the man took Sunday drives. They no longer had evenings out in the resort hotels but they traversed the country roads that he loved, passing brooks and streams that he would return to alone with his fishing equipment and friends.

As she carried in her belly the unborn child, she fixed her gaze on the children they passed along the roadways—the country children—to see what she could find of her own childhood in their faces, what she might have brought from the past to the infant in her womb.

They came toward the car along the side of the highway—skirts too long, coats too short, shoes, if any, too big; an infant with a bony head in the arms of the oldest girl, or walking beside her, hand in hers, just a step too far onto the macadam for a driver's comfort. They had stick candy in their mouths or Nu Grape soda purpling their tongues. The smallest-size paper sack, its top twisted shut, its contents the spongy, sticky sweets of the poor, was clutched tightly in the baby's fist. The child wore an empty, vacant look, and into its features Flora read a dawning familiarity with infinite sorrow.

They would have made their purchases with warm coins. Flora remembered herself as a child coming to know each coin personally and giving it up with the same feelings of sadness and loss that followed the mattress-piled pickup truck turning onto the highway carrying away another friend.

The coins were held in the palm, at the soul center of the hand, and lingered in impression even after they had been placed on the storekeeper's counter. They didn't stay on the counter long; he was eager to get them, to spill them rapidly into the hand-cranked cash register, its pocket-filled, fat-sow mouth shoved open to receive them.

It had been the same when Minnie spent a bill, Flora remembered. Folding money. Minnie contemplated the goods, turning them in her hands, her face rigid, before she withdrew the money from the purse within her purse. She smoothed the bills length-wise in her hands again and again, as if to separate the ones into further ones, as though with sufficient stroking they would shed their skins like snakes and leave a reasonable reproduction of themselves behind.

They came toward the car along the highway, the country children, leaving behind them the filling station–general store, clotted flypaper swaying in the breeze from the torn screen door, flyswatter on the counter, flyspecks on the glass.

The children walk on dirt packed hard as concrete–dead, red dirt. On rocks, pebbles. Flocks of starlings precede them, swooping down to peck grit for their craws. The children are pierced in the eyes, blinded momentarily by the glint of sun on broken glass. Recovering, they read the collections of gutters, the tossed rubbish of automobile passengers. Their hair blows when the man's car overtakes them, their eyes squint in the wind. But their looks don't follow the car, Flora observes.

They walk past mailboxes. Past straggly forsythia in spring, then "flags," the country name for iris. Then, as time passes, they walk in the cold hard light of winter Sunday.

They don't talk much, country children. Or ask questions. They already know.

IT was a girl. It was pale and cold and thin and blue but it breathed.

Flora, who had had a difficult delivery, lay in the same hospital where she had gone for the nurse's training she had never finished. Her former classmates, giggling, popped in to see her. They turned and left quietly if the man was there, made excuses to linger if it was the boy who visited.

For several days Flora breast-fed the child, until it was discovered that the infant sucked on emptiness. The man had the baby taken from the common nursery and placed in a private room with attendants around the clock. The staff panicked under his frown and hastened to replenish by way of bottle feedings the too-rapid weight loss in the already frail being. For a time they thought that there was a deficiency in the heartbeat of the tiny girl but later decided not.

As the fuss was being made over the baby—the formula, the cleansing of hands, wearing of masks—Flora remembered the slovenly pigpen of a cabin where their farm neighbor, Jessie Garnley, lived and gave birth to her many children, not one of whom resembled the other. Jessie was a slattern, and Flora had heard the children called "cabbage-patch babies." Some nights Jessie could be seen out wandering behind barns or down the highway toward a parked pickup truck. It was said she was not right in her mind. The men who hunkered down outside the general store said she might be crazy in the head but from the neck down she made pretty good sense.

Her children, overalls stiff with soil, earth and human, whined and crept away from the husband, old man Garnley with his wooden leg.

Years back Garnley had run over his own foot with his plow but kept working, and at the end of the day when he got home hadn't even washed the cut. Some days after, Jessie in her desultory fashion wandered up to the Rawlingses' to complain about Garnley losing his mind and stinking.

Minnie went to have a look and found him raving with fever and pain, maggots silently architecting passages in what had been flesh. She made Rawlings hitch up the wagon and drive Garnley to the county hospital, where they managed to save his life after sawing off his rotten limb.

Garnley held Minnie responsible for the loss of his leg. Flora and her sisters were told never to get too near his house, there was no telling what he might do in revenge.

Flora sensed this to be true. She had seen a look in Garnley's eyes when he stared at a female. A look that spoke not to the individual but to the species. A call, eons in regress, primeval, urgent, repellent. She saw black places described in that glance, unencountered but known.

THERE was ice on the ground the day Flora came home from the hospital. The man drove the car and she sat beside him. A uniformed practical nurse, holding the baby, crackled in starched perfection in the rear.

When the car pulled up to the front of the stone house Randolf came down the walk. The man got out of the car and helped Flora to a wobbly standing position. Randolf put his arm around her waist. The man left them and went toward the house, up the broad front walk, where he then stood, waiting, the front door held open. Randolf moved his arm upward from Flora's waist to the middle of her back. The other arm gently collapsed the joint of her knee. She buckled and sank into his grasp. He straightened up, holding her, her own arm around his neck. The skirt of her flowing robe—she had not been permitted to dress—fell to his midleg and moved with the breeze of his walk as he carried her into the house.

The man, a small figure, still wearing his hat, followed them up the stairway to the master bedroom.

Randolf carried Flora to the ivory-and-blue bed. The sheets on her side had been folded back to form a neat triangle, the pillows propped up for her to lean against. Randolf put a knee onto the bed to brace his weight, leaned over and placed Flora on the covers. He released her. She released him.

Then Randolf went back to the car to escort the nurse and baby up the treacherous walk.

THREE

 I LOST one of the twins. It was the one with brown eyes, too. Almost all my singles had blue eyes so when I got the twins I had particularly wanted one with brown eyes and one with blue so that I could tell them apart. I wanted twins because it seemed to me that most things came in pairs. Shoes and socks, mothers and fathers, blacks and whites, girls and boys, good and bad, dogs and cats (although that didn't really count), and so on.

Order had become important. I placed things—books, boxes—in descending order. Small on top, larger and larger going down. I arranged dishes in a straight line on the table with my left hand as I ate with my right. Threw my weight behind upholstered pieces of furniture to shove and align them with the floorboards or the patterns in the rug. I was made uneasy by the random design in some of the carpets and studied them hoping to detect a system. I had impulses to draw the window shades to the exact same height in all the windows of the house and found myself going out of doors and walking the perimeters of the dwelling to check them, then returning and climbing stairs to fix those that were a fraction off.

I tidied the crayons in their box, my desk at school, the towels on the towel bars in our bathrooms.

It soothed me to put things in pairs. Either the same or opposite, matching or opposed.

I wanted to have in my clothing chest at any given time the same number of undervests as bloomers. And an equal number of pairs of socks. I wanted my clothes for the next day laid out at night in a certain order on a chair placed in a certain way.

I got out of bed three times a night to make sure the closet door was tightly shut. It had to be three separate times or I was unable to rest. I felt that some punishment would come to me, some harm.

When I finally found the missing twin she was in our cellar. Her face had crackled into tiny lines and her soft body smelled of earth. One of the brown eyes refused to open. All summer and into the autumn while she had been in the cellar I had wheeled the blue-eyed one in a baby buggy, had dressed her and fed her tea parties at Caroline's house and shampooed her stiff hair, even though I had been told not to.

I MUST have left the brown-eyed one in the cellar when I was watching Sadie do the wash.

Laundry was done on Monday in a Siamese pair of large white enamel tubs up on legs against the basement wall. Sadie filled one tub with water and whipped up a cream of suds. It was soothing to hear the water gush and gurgle and to watch the floating bubbles and their reflections. It gave me space for my own reflections on the day before. I thought of what Sundays had become.

A washboard was Sadie's only tool. That and her powerful dark arms, hands and wrists. She took up each item, examined it for serious dirt or stains, and then, after giving it its own individual application of bar soap, scrubbed it up and down over the tin furrows of the washboard.

Sadie was very proud that she could plunge her hands into steaming water for the first soaping. Local opinion held that the only way to get clothes *clean* was to boil them over a fire outdoors. Second best was to wash them in as near to boiling water as would not actually remove skin from bone. This was Sadie's method.

Next she reached into the rinse, withdrew a piece of clothing and with her mighty upper arms spread out and her elbows bent, wrenched the garment into opposite directions against its own center until all drops of water had been wrung out. It seemed to me that she did this with particular vigor to my father's clothes.

Sadie was not a pretty woman. And sometimes she frightened me with stories of stabbings on The Hill and talk about eyes rolling up into people's heads and never reappearing and old women who laid on curses. She was not at all jolly like her sister, Lo, who came one day and taught me the Big Apple, a dance with rubber-legged movements, all the while talking about Joe Louis and how much she loved him. "He's my man!" Lo said. "He's my man!"

Sadie had to have been married at some point, I reasoned. Because of Lily Mae. I felt that the name Lily Mae had been given in the hope that the girl would turn white, like the laundry, if worked over sufficiently. But I saw no evidence of a husband and wondered if Sadie felt the lack.

The hot water for the washing was heated by Alexander. He arrived even earlier on Monday than he did other days. He had a hand that tried to touch his elbow, the result of a wound from the War, and the reason he got befuddled in the head, my mother told me, was because he had been gassed.

I asked Sadie if she would like to marry Alexander. She shot me a withering glance and said, "He gots a woman." She went on under her breath, and I caught fragments. "Some peoples . . . and thinks . . . they goins on not notice . . . Ah sees . . . !"

Her displeasure on any topic caused me to rush into self-examination, but at the same time she seldom gave me sufficient clues to pin down the crime.

WHEN I found the mildewed doll there in the cellar it made me think of Cousin Sally's baby. My mother said that her Cousin Sally was "created middle-aged" and had never been a day younger and would never seem a day older her whole life long.

I remembered that when she came home from the hospital my mother and I went to visit. There in a pretty crib next to Garth and Sally's bed was a tiny squinch-faced boy. I knew that I would have been supremely happy to have soft little blankets and drawstring nightgowns and giant diaper pins to work with all day long, but Sally had tears in her eyes and we didn't stay long. On the way home my mother told me there had been two babies, twins, but one had died.

He died but he came to all the birthday parties anyway. Whenever one of the cousins had a birthday, Sally would arrive holding one little boy by the hand and it always seemed to me that her other hand held something, too. She would lead the child toward us, tell him to join our games, and then I would see —but not be sure I'd seen—Sally, with the slightest forward move-ment of her empty hand, urge the other, invisible little boy toward us, too.

My twins were nothings. Dolls were all either girls or noth-ings. Usually the ones with hard bodies were girls and the ones with soft bodies were nothings. They were never boys, which was what I really wanted to see. It was strange that they didn't make dolls of the most important kind of person there was to be; I didn't understand that. Maybe it would give away a kind of magic that they didn't want everybody to know, because then most people would choose to be boys and it wouldn't work out right anymore about the pairs.

Caroline had a woman doll. It was not all bloated like the baby dolls; it had two peaks on its chest. Its waist went in and its hips went out. I became feverish when she let me hold it and take its corset off and wrap it in a feather boa. It had a face just like a little girl's, though, not a grown-up's, and it looked funny in stockings. I would go home slightly ill from those afternoons. My mother noticed and then made Sadie take me for a walk the next afternoon after school rather than dropping me off at Caroline's house to play.

We walked to the First Baptist Church, a hideous, red, crouching structure surrounded by a low retaining wall. All the nursemaids of the neighborhood gathered here in the afternoons to compare their ironing and their gossip. The ironing was displayed on the squirming body of whatever child the maid pushed in its giant carriage. The gossip was revealed later.

While the child had napped the maid had chosen and prepared its wardrobe, dampened the heavily starched garment, and ironed it to board-stiff perfection. Then the child was bathed and, still doped and groggy from day-sleep, buttoned, tied, laced, combed, pinned, fluffed, buckled, wrapped, and secured into pinafore, sunsuit, or party dress, depending on final destination. The "good" children were those torpid creatures with no will or spirit who could be bullied with a dark glance into immobility. Dire futures were predicted for all others.

I was in school now and partially released from that familiar bondage. Instead of standing or sitting comatose, I was permitted a balancing walk on top of the low wall with Sadie gripping my hand, back and forth for two trips. But I knew the rules. When Cyrus pedaled by we had to stop. All the nursemaids gathered in a bunch to see where he was headed.

He delivered for the drugstore. They all watched to see if he was going to Tansy's house.

Tansy was in my grade at school. Her mother was the adult version of Snow White: ivory skin, ebony hair that formed a point in the middle of her forehead, and just as Snow White slept for years, so did Tansy's mother travel though life in a semisomnolent state. I never heard her say more than three words. She proceeded, sublime, enigmatic, and smoldering with her own private concerns—or lack of them, who could tell?—while the rest of the world troubled itself with its own interpretations of what her feelings and emotions surely must be.

Most afternoons all the mothers I knew put on their flowered voile dresses and took turns going to each other's houses to play bridge. Tansy's mother let it be known that she didn't play cards. She wore pale silk blouses and dark skirts. She went somewhere else in the afternoons. Nobody ever said where. Whenever she was out, Tansy was allowed to order a melted pimento cheese sandwich and a milkshake from the drugstore.

When the maids saw Cyrus ring Tansy's bell they all shook their heads slowly and smiled. One of them would say, "Huh, huh, *huh. Somebody* a happy man today." I didn't think they meant Tansy's father. He never seemed happy. He was always nervous and he had a silly mustache.

On Wednesdays I tapped. My mother picked me up after school, bringing with her my shoes and practice clothes in a suitcase, and dropped me at the studio. In the car on the way to class I opened the case and checked to see that I had everything I needed. It was humiliating to get there and find that I missed one ribbon tie, or the tights or slippers still silver-gilt from the recital last spring.

I climbed out of the car followed by washes of Flora's discontent. Waves of it, strong and silent, so that when I turned to close the car door I set down my case in order to shove against the tide with both hands, arms stiff, palms against cold steel.

For the recital, each student had been a flower. Caroline an iris, Tansy a pink, I a daffodil. I adored my costume although it made me itch. It had unfinished seams all up and down the inside of the tightly fitted bodice, and as I moved the raw edges tormented me like rows of fierce crawling ants in marching order, their shiny black mandibles snipping at my rib cage.

In preparation for the recital, several seamstresses were hired and sat in the anteroom of the dance studio handling such stuffs as chiffon, braid, artificial flowers, velvet ribbons. They ran elastic through leg and waist of shiny satin underpants, gathered layer upon layer of stiff pink net for ballet skirts, nestling a velvet pansy or organdy tea rose here and there in the folds. They cut lengths of taffeta ribbon for each pair of taps that we were to wear and entrusted us to poke them through the eyelets of the shoes.

For the recital we wore lipstick! And rouge! Child faces turned into hoydens, the recital hall suddenly the seraglio of some potentate who delighted in child wantons.

The flower dresses were for the ballet number. For the tap routine we did a schoolroom dance in white satin skirt and top with bare midriff. The skirt had letters of the alphabet in red spangles pasted on. The scenery was a giant blackboard on which simple words and sums had been painted. It was an "exam" in which the dancer playing the teacher and holding a long pointer instructed us, and we tapped out in formation and in time to rollicking music various letters and words and answered addition and subtraction problems by stamping our feet.

The real teacher wanted to have one dancer play the dunce and sit on a high stool with a pointed cap on her head as punishment for giving wrong answer taps. The students were indignant. The question unsettled, we all went home, outraged, to complain to our mothers. The teacher had to forego her comic relief. There had been a terrible moment, though, as I explained the situation to Flora, as I described the schoolroom test, when a musing, vacant look came over her face and I truly feared she might make me take the part.

I learned the dance routines rapidly. They appealed to me with their patterns and repeated movements, each growing logically out of the one before. We learned the steps by repetition and by saying the names of them over and over as we did the moves. "Hop shuffle step, shuffle, ball *change*." And on "ball *change*" there was a smart smacking sound that gave definition and exclamation to the moves that had come before, as though we had reached some high point that was worth rejoicing about in a ringing, metallic congratulation.

The dance studio was upstairs over a dry-cleaning establishment, so that as we hopped and turned we breathed in the pungent smell of the solvent they used. Whenever my father's clean suits were delivered to our house it made me think of dancing class. If I passed his clothes closet and caught a whiff of the chemical, dance memories popped into my mind.

Lucille Vandalla taught all the classes herself. She was a dynamo of muscular energy. She wore shorts for tap and for ballet she wrapped a brief skirt around her waist. Black bangs slashed her forehead, heavy-rimmed glasses outlined her fringed, farsighted eyes, pistons drove her ankles and calves. She was not married. As she tapped or did pliés before us, our eyes riveted to her perfection, I attempted to conjure up her private life.

Lucille Vandalla led us through routines of sailor dances, milkmaid dances, minuets, a Spanish fandango, mincing Japanese toe-ins, hearty polkas. Revealing to us in sketched, abbreviated gesture—a toss of her head, a shrug of her expressive shoulder—the very essence of vocation, history and national character, both East and West.

I thought about her on days other than my class and in the hours before and after I was there. She was dancing all day every day. I was confounded at the number of miles she traveled in that studio, both literal and figurative. Leaping in one room but interpreting the world.

She lived in a white, two-story brick building that had four apartments. Her private entry door could be seen from the street. The public could actually walk past her dwelling and see her *door*. I expected it to pulsate. Even explode. I didn't understand how the town could contain her, why it didn't burst into flame and consume itself and burn to the ground in homage around her, leaving her standing alone in her tap shorts in the center of a vast ring of scorched earth.

IN regular school I liked the way numbers could take different partners and still add up to the identical sum. Each number took on a personality for me, and I remembered the combinations of them with pleasure. Five was chubby. Three was a baby holding out its arms. Four, on the other hand, was a dependable, business sort. Seven was tall and skinny. Eight was a fun-loving creature. The ten sequences were simple-minded and dull. Nine was tricky and almost always brought with it the burden of "carrying."

When I tired of the number pairs I worked on the people.

Kenny Whitfield made a pair with his mother. They were both blond and beautiful. When he had to leave her to start school with the rest of us, she couldn't bear to cut his curls. Also she dressed him in blue suits with short pants. All the other boys wore corduroy knickers that went switch, switch.

Because she missed him so much all day she bought him both a pony wagon and a goat cart and took turns driving them to school, waiting out front for him at release time. Then he would take over the reins and go "Cheek, cheek" from the side of his mouth, and they trotted home together.

The first grade girls thought he was beautiful and wanted to comb his hair. The boys shoved him and pushed him on stairs so that his naked knees were always scabby. When he had a very bad day, no matter which rig his mother brought, it was the wrong one. But he never let his mother know he was suffering on her account—because of how she made him look. When she drove up with, for instance, the pony wagon, Kenny would raise a tiny clenched fist and stamp his Mary Janes on the walk of the school. He would shriek from his blazing red face, "Momma! Why didn't you bring the goddamned *goat* cart!?" Tears would slide from his mother's lashes.

Horace was new, and at first, because he was strange, I thought he could make a pair with Kenny. Horace had a terrible slack mouth and he pinched people. We all hated him, including the teacher. One day she let us begin to beat him up. We all crowded around and closed in on him and smiled and began to hit as hard as we could. It made me feel just the same as when I played with the woman doll. But then the teacher pretended she hadn't meant it and began to yell at us and pull us away. But I knew she had meant it.

The teacher was a one. She was an old maid. It was easy to see why. She had gray hair. Also, all day long she cleared her throat and spit things into a handkerchief. She was not a pair but she had her milk. Every day during arithmetic someone from the lunchroom tiptoed in and left a little bottle of milk on her desk. As she stood at the blackboard, all during numbers, she would glance at it, an excited sparkle in her eyes. The milk grew warmer and warmer as it sat in the body-smelling classroom. During story hour she would slowly sip it from a straw and read to us and spit. Everybody went home from first grade and gagged on milk and cookies.

JUST as numbers added up to tidy and dependable sums, I felt that humans in their family groups ought to be put together neatly, too. Just as there was a sort of carpentry for numerals—a joining, splicing, beveling—so should there be a proper fitting, a trimness in the combinations of mankind.

I had a vision that there was an ideal family, but I didn't know quite how I evolved it or what I wanted it to be: what the ages of the parents should be, the number of children they should have, how they passed their calm, happy hours together. In reality everybody had something about their family that made it different from other families.

Minnie and Rawlings had ten children. That was unusual.

Cousin Sally and Garth had lost a baby. That was not common. In a house down the street lived a family with one beautiful child, a little girl. She had been born with all her fingers adhering together in a knobbed, bulbous clump.

In those last families the difference was Sadness. Another category I headed Living Arrangements.

Just as Randolf had lived in with my family, my classmate Sue-anne's grandmother lived in with her—a patrician old lady, arthritic and crippled, but proper and regal just the same. Once, while I was at Sue-anne's, the old lady fell. We heard the tumbling thud and her groan. There were only the two of us and the grandmother in the house. We rushed to her room.

Sue-anne gasped. I knew, with sinking heart, what she would say next.

"You stay here with Granny . . . you watch her while I call my father home from work!"

The naked old lady had fallen on all fours and remained that way, hands and knees on the bare floor, looking up at me. I stood in her doorway, an inadequate, mortified and helpless attendant. We both knew it was terribly wrong for me to see her this way, but we both also knew I had to be there to record and be ready to report further collapse. I heard Sue-anne's voice on the phone. The old lady and I continued to gaze at each other. She moaned. What could I do? A wet stain appeared on the floor. Drops of yellow water fell, it seemed, from her abdomen. The urine, before dripping to the floor, trickled along a path toward her navel and then spilled.

Later, I wondered what my own mother would look like when she was an old lady. How her face would wrinkle up and her skin get all powdery and seem to sift into my mouth as I kissed her. Old ladies had spreading brown splotches on their skin, liver spots that mapped and disfigured once flawless unclaimed open territory—the free states, the unhomesteaded regions, the fresh meadows, moist and smooth, of young girls, smelling of sun and air and wild flowers. I tried to impose an old-lady smell on Flora. I sniffed for lavender sachets, for that manless-house smell of the apartments of old ladies. That noticeable absence of the mating smell—seldom remarked in its presence, but the human nose is startled, wounded, affronted by its absence. I imposed these conditions on Flora. I tied on her feet the sturdy-heeled, arch-supporting, perforated black shoes of age. I draped around her neck the shawls of aged bedtime. I placed by her bed a drinking glass with bent tube straw . . . I puffed up her slender ankles, took a brushstroke of flesh from her thighs and streaked it across her shoulders, I thickened her middle, sagged her breasts, tumored her abdomen, but none of it stayed. None of it stuck. Flora sloughed it off. I tried it again and again but Flora dodged it, she refused it; no matter with what strength of vision I applied the images in my mind, they didn't adhere. I could not age Flora. At a certain point, time stood still.

So, with some families it was Living Arrangements that were out of the ordinary. With others, it was Sadness. Even more unsettling than these events—which seemed visited on people helpless to their fate—were Behavior Aberrations. Disturbing acts that appeared to be matters of deliberate choice.

Some were minor things such as Miss Chadwick filling her rank house with smelly dogs.

Dogs could have made perfect companions except for several unfortunate flaws. The way they were forced to attend to personal hygiene was one of God's mistakes. I felt sure that the intelligence Who had given us tulips and sunsets and butterflies could have produced a more acceptable approach to personal daintiness and, for that matter, communication than the ones dogs were forced to live with. It was probably one of the miscellaneous things that had been cleared up hurriedly near the end of the six days of creation.

"Let's see, birds will splash in rain puddles to bathe . . . elephants will spray themselves with their trunks—that's a good one, I *like* that," God said to Himself. "Now for dogs. What will I do there? What haven't I used yet?" Pause for thinking. "I've got it! Tongues! I'll have dogs bathe with their tongues!"

It troubled me further that the dogs didn't seem to be put off by the system. That, in fact, instead of seldom and reluctantly attending to baths, they often washed longer than the dictates of mere cleanliness would have demanded.

However, owning too many dogs was a minor thing. There were people who did major, unspeakable things.

My mother's friend, Trudy, had a boisterous son. A child turbulent, threatening, rough, monstrous. He had the curled, tousled hair and Dresden-china face of an angel.

Once, the two mothers left us together in Trudy's car while they popped into a store on an errand. As she left the car Trudy pointed her finger at the boy and said, "Now you behave, and you *know* what I mean!" The second they were out of sight he hopped out of the car and right there on Lanier Street pulled down his pants and wobbled his private parts at the people on the sidewalk.

I was aghast. Horrified. He would read with delight the building smile of some approaching lady beginning to notice his facial beauty and wait for the delicious moment when the passerby—now upon him—saw his antics for what they were, gasped, and hurried away. The climax of his fun came when the outraged woman looked back and pierced the window of the car with a dagger at *me*, as though *I* were responsible!

How I longed for his death.

And as for what he had on his body that he was so roundly displaying, *that* was an accumulation of organic horrors to annihilate lucid thought.

I had been curious about boys, it was true. But only for some discreet, removed, more technical kind of information. Something diagramed in a book, not even necessarily in color, for I now saw that even the helpless—though obscene—hue of the living object overwhelmed me. This repugnance represented an act of creation both mischievous and whimsical.

My glimpse, through eyes glazed over by shock, showed me that the male had a front beset with numbers of tubes and pouches—it was hard to tell just how many—all ajiggle in different directions. How could the gender even walk? It must be a constant experience of rearrangement and disarray.

Whenever I looked at my own body I saw that it went straight down a front decorated only by two spots on the chest and a tidy belly button, it paused a moment, and then curved under. There were some complications, true, but these were neatly and thoughtfully placed so as not to alarm the eye of the viewer. Then the entire business rose up on the other side and became, with no fuss at all, the back.

How could males ride horses? bicycles? Fight wars? With all those things to account for and distribute.

The pouches were sagging, wizened, poorly designed containers for some roundish objects. They were loosely gathered into a pair and held up in the middle by some sort of vein or sinew between them. The more forward, prominent tube bobbed and dipped dopily from side to side, seeming both stunned and vagrant. The overall impression was of terrible disorder. Of a cruel humiliating mistake that any halfway sane person would do his utmost to keep always and forever hidden and out of sight.

THE autumn rains came, turning the leaves of the pin oaks belly-up. Crisp air scoured the lungs, maples and frost made love and glowed. I was taken to try on winter coats, one for school, the other for church and parties. The pool at the country club was drained and the golfers became poker players. My mother bought wool in crimson and black for a new suit.

The late afternoon hours were now especially empty ones for her. She walked from window to window idly, puttered in the kitchen as Sadie prepared dinner, came home from her bridge later and later, arriving at the front door just as my father entered at the back.

When she did stay home and play cards by herself I sat near her with a book which I didn't read but held to keep myself looking busy and to control my tendency to crowd too close to her as she played.

She handled the cards with ownership. They were her creatures. They had life when she chose to give it to them for a few minutes late in the afternoon. She laid them out crisply, causing each one to snap onto the table by a final flick of her nail under its corner. They were played out in parade rows, awaiting her inspection and attention.

I had the impression as they lay there on the table under her examination that they actually smartened up.

There was a game of solitaire that was laid out in the form of a pyramid. It was chipped away bit by bit as she played. Eventually, in a speeded-up version of the erosion of time, the pyramid became a ruin.

She pulled the cards toward her to shuffle, gazing out the window as she did so. Her hands knew their work alone, unguided. She looked at the birds fluttering and hopping in the bare trees and shrubs outside the window. A sparrow plummeted to earth for a seed in a move so final that it seemed the creature would surely dash the brain from its tiny skull. But then, with the least widening of its wings—a move more decision than aerodynamics—it took command of the fall, righted itself, and picked the seed with a nip of its beak.

"I think birds were happier before there was man," Flora said, not really to me, more toward me. "The grass was taller then. They didn't have to land on this bald, brown, mown stuff and be all nervous looking around for their enemies. Nobody went carrying on about the little cracked shells fallen from the nest or thought of using robins as a sign of spring or that kind of nonsense. Birds seem almost more like ornaments now than what they really are. Which is just birds."

There must have been billions of them in a planetary aviary—scattering the clouds, air-swimming in rain. There was no one to mark their journeys, to count their migrations. They flew the world for their own concerns. The grass was lush, a sweet green forest heavy with seed; plants bent to their beaks, with each seed an atom of dew. They took food and drink in security.

A horizon of birds, breasts burnished by the primeval gold-red sun, hovered, stopped, and the air stopped with them, halted by a wall of outstretched wings. They settled and slept. At dawn a thousand songs mingled and ten thousand hearts each pulsed an ounce of blood into a fingertip heart. The birds rose. And if each bird lost only one feather, I thought, then plume, down, and quill would drift to earth and create an ever-moving, ever-changing jeweled carpet below.

"PART of the reason I'm so depressed," my mother said to my father at dinner one night, "is that I have to depend on my friends for rides. I only have the car one day, Wednesday, and I have to do everything in that one afternoon. Drop her at dance class," a nod at me, "look for my fabric, grocery shop and everything. I always have to be picked up by Trudy or someone for the card games."

"Good Lord," said my father. "The cheapest new car you can buy has *got* to be over six hundred dollars."

"Christmas is coming. I thought maybe a car might be what I'd want for Christmas."

"Closer to seven hundred the way these bandits add on the extras. That's some present."

My mother began to shop for cars anyway.

My parents had spent every Sunday afternoon drive of the autumn arguing. We started out to where we were headed, sometimes to my grandparents' house, but more often for a trip into the mountains, and they began as the wheels started to roll. They seemed compelled to work through the arguments as they drove over the same roads and up the same winding curves they had traversed while courting.

As my father's temper became more and more inflamed, he drove closer and closer to the median divider until, at moments of extreme stress, the entire left side of the car settled in a state of ownership in the lane devoted to oncoming traffic. I could see the instant of startled surprise and stunned disbelief on the face of the driver hurtling toward us as he perceived the situation.

My father took the curves of the mountain roads not by moving the steering wheel in one smooth operation but by turning a bit, then sliding his hands to the crest of the circle, turning and sliding, so that each curve was executed in a series of jerks and lurches.

Then, if we were low on gas, he would streak out into the wilderness, choosing a crossroads where there was no sign of human habitation, leaving my mother in a panic that we would be stranded, fuelless for hours in strange country.

There were endless "but you *said*"s and "well, then, why didn't *you*"s, followed by sharp digs, none of which ever exhumed the source of the disagreement. In fact, no matter what it was they began arguing about, the end result was the same repeated series of condemnations, of set pieces that occurred over and over again.

I sagged in the backseat, silent party to these episodes, a necessary monitor of some sort because they waited for this time to go at each other. The cigarette smoke as both of them lit and puffed and exhaled swirled and filled the car, making me sicker and sicker.

My father, as he got engrossed in the argument, missed turns, swerving back to make them after he had passed the intersection, causing the cars and trucks behind him no end of consternation. Then came the sounding of horns, the shriek of tires halted in midrevolution. My mother gasped and clutched the armrest on her side of the door, flinching involuntarily. She rode, on these occasions, with her body tilting to the right, as though by willing her thoughts and exerting the density of her substance to the right she could somehow influence the car and encourage it into its correct lane.

My father drove faster and faster, the voices grew more and more furious, the car wove and careened.

Finally he found a gas station and jerked the car to a stop with a stamp on the foot brake and a virtual uprooting of the emergency.

The inserting of the gasoline-hose nozzle into the tank propelled him from the car. With a change of mood so swift as to be unbelievable, he began to chat amiably with the attendant about crops or the weather, presented me with a grape soda or a melty Popsicle for which all appetite had long since been demolished. My mother sat, fuming and teary, in the front seat, enclosed in her private shell of bitterness.

CHRISTMAS came and went. My father gave my mother a black kidskin purse. To go with her new suit, he told her. Randolf sent me a scooter. I felt guilty in my vehicle ownership as I glided up and down the sidewalk in front of the house.

The Sunday after Christmas she refused to get into the car for the afternoon drive. She said, not very convincingly, that she had a headache, and went off upstairs with a novel.

My father looked up the stairs toward her retreating back. Then he looked down at me.

"Come on," he said.

I got into the front seat beside him.

It was a gray day, cold, characterless.

He took a different route. We did not head into the country but drove instead past his mill. It was closed, of course, on Sunday. Only the man who fired the boiler was there, standing in the door of the firehouse for a breath of air.

My father raised his hand in silent salute. The fellow waved back. He was a shaggy, barrel-chested man. The firehouse sat in the mill yard, and the chimney stack rose skyward beside it. The ground of the lot was bare of vegetation and covered with cinders, residue of the coal the boiler fed on. Usually the old man with his grimy fingernails and whiskery chin sat outside on a broken-down wooden chair with a sly grin on his face watching the mill girls as they came and went.

"Does he live there?" I asked my father.

"Hard to say."

After we passed the mill he drove by his other properties—a four-story office building in the block next to the one where the mill was situated, then over toward the tracks to pull into the lot of his warehouse, pause, and then back out. Each building was closed and silent in the quiet of Sunday afternoon.

Then to the old side of town where he owned some rental houses, wood-frame, the porches and steps beginning to show their age. In one front yard a single strand of rope hung from a bare tree and was looped around a worn black automobile tire to make a swing. A rusting red wagon, its handle dropped askew on the cracked cement walk, held a naked doll.

After we visited his properties he drove out to the edge of town and passed the other mills. Some of the bigger factories had mill housing, rows of mongrels with their backs nestled into the belly and sides of the rangy brick factory itself, or lined up along the spur rails, or tossed in ragged rows up the hillside across the road. The large mills spit fluff and dye into the downhill stream that uphill, fresh and clean, gave them power. The mill houses were four rooms, two over two, bulging with humanity.

I supposed that he was thinking about Randolf and the mill where he had taken a job down in South Carolina. Randolf had written that it was "sizable."

I MISSED Randolf and our talks about words. One day before he had even said he was leaving we had had a talk about words and definitions.

I saved up my questions for him, words that I had heard and that puzzled me, for rainy days when we sat at the dining-room table together with our paperwork.

"Randolf, what does *ward* mean?"

"I expect you've been hearing our father talk about politics. For voting purposes, towns and cities are divided into sections called 'wards.' Is that it?"

"No. I don't think so. It's about a person. Some kind of person."

"A ward heeler? Was that the use of the word? Or as an action, as in one who wards off harm or evil? That sort of thing?"

"No. It was Trudy talking. She said you were my mother's 'young ward.' What does that mean?"

Silence. I was confident that he knew the meaning. He was phrasing his answer. I waited patiently.

"She has misused the word."

Randolf hadn't finished. He wanted to say more. I waited again.

"She has misused the word, and it's an embarrassing misuse. I would be grateful if you did not carry this question elsewhere."

Puzzling. I wondered if Randolf were moving into that adult world where all true communication ceased.

"How about a 'smoking jacket'? Tansy's father has a 'smoking jacket.' What's that?" I tested.

Randolf snorted. "He would. He would, wouldn't he?" But he told me. I was disappointed. I had thought the garment actually smoldered.

Just a few weeks after that, Randolf said he had written for a job down in South Carolina. My father was enraged until Randolf explained that in order to know how to beat the competition he had to have some experience in the ways other mills did things. And so he left.

I STUDIED the mill children as we passed them along the side of the road and wondered if they were the same where Randolf was. The babies all looked sad.

When the boys reached adolescence they grew tough and mean-spirited with slit eyes and greasy clumped hair. They played vicious ball and used knives in brawls after the games.

The girls were either slutty or ugly, wan bonebags.

It was told about the mill women and girls how on sharp winter nights they would urinate into the coal bucket to avoid a trip to the outdoor privy and then wear the black ring of coal dust on their cheeks till Saturday bath night.

Summers, in the steaming mill, they would go without underpants and risk (or invite) the eyes of the men workers up through cracked floorboards of the stairs.

Some houses were heated with kerosene stoves, and the people who lived in them always smelled of the oily fluid. The stoves were called "portable" although when lifted they sloshed their flammable contents onto the clothing of the porter and onto the floors of the wooden house. Many mill hands had shiny, puckered scars where the flesh had grazed a hot stove, or a slick side of the face where a tongue of flame had been slaked.

We drove into the darkening afternoon at times retracing our path so as to pass each mill and factory in town and even those out of town on the highway.

Several of the houses had a quarantine notice tacked to the door. I thought I would surely die if ever I got sick and they did that to our house. Inside someone had scarlet fever or measles or whooping cough. Mill people were thought to be a raging source of contagious illness, a breeding ground of infestation.

I imagined the sick child behind the door, lying on a bed, rickety iron bars of head- and foot-board chipped, paint peeling. The child would have been placed in the parents' room when it got ill to keep it from infecting the other two or three children with whom it ordinarily slept. The child lay, tossing with fever or shivering with chills, sweat seeping into the mattress that had received the dews of love, childbirth, and death many times before.

Or the child bent, coughing, turning first red and then blue as it struggled with the phlegms and fluids that lay between its air passages and the oxygen they strived to take in. It was the hour of meal preparation. The heads of the other members of the family began to turn as the struggle prolonged. They halted in their tasks of table setting or slicing fatback or snapping beans, to watch, almost idly, the battle. To witness, perhaps, the triumph of death over tiny lungs.

After we had seen all the factories—hosiery, twine, cotton goods, even furniture—my father, at last, headed back toward town. We returned to lawns and churches and to streets laid out in blocks.

We didn't drive straight home, however. He drove slowly past the closed, locked showrooms of the automobile dealers first and peered through the big windows of plate glass at the shadowed cars inside.

We did not mention or discuss a summing-up moral precept for that day.

IT seemed a flagrant impropriety to see cars indoors, under a roof in a place where there were desks and chairs and carpets. But there they were, placed artfully around the big showroom, some heading one way, some another. If they had been moving and on the road, they surely would all have crashed into each other and spoiled their shiny paint and crushed their bulbous eye sockets.

"How do you get them in here?" I managed to lodge the question between torrents of sales talk.

The man did not pause in his cascade and, without looking either at me or in the direction at which he pointed, stuck a finger out toward a set of double doors from the back lot.

I studied them. Sure enough. If both were thrown open, a car could be driven through. I yearned for the job. The slight aura of wrongness, naughtiness, about it appealed to me mightily. A forbidden sort of act for which one would be both admired and paid. "Did you see how she got that big sedan through those doors without putting a scratch on it? Whew! That was a close one." Then, beaming at me, "You sure have an eye!" And they rushed to shake my hand.

My mother gravitated toward a two-door dark red coupe. It had a regular front seat, but the rear was less cushy and crowded the two (tops) passengers close together. To get into the back one had to squeeze behind the front seat as it was held forward and, clinging with one hand, monkey fashion, to the strap handle, lower the buttocks onto the seat. It was easy for me, but my mother fretted about her bridge friends mussing their dresses as they pushed in. Or if they were done up for afternoon tea they might tilt their hats awry.

I knew she had a budget, but I could also foresee freedom from further trips with Trudy's freak of a son. I silently urged her toward purchase.

As they talked I crept into the backseat again. I felt a fondness for it and already a kind of ownership. That was where I traveled. I noticed the pouch pockets stitched to the rear of each front seat and thought of them as repositories for my crayons and books. The back windows were rounded triangles, portholes that swiveled open and closed with a handled latch. Embedded in the armrest on each side was a lidded ashtray so small that to use it would require not only strong motivation but deadly aim. I knew the smoking habits of my mother's friends. They were heedless.

On the wall just to the stern of the doorframe was the light switch. It didn't flick up and down as a house lighting fixture did but was a minute sliding piece, grooved, so that even a fingertip could find purchase. When the light was turned on it glowed through its marbleized celluloid cover with a transfixing warm beam that satisfied some longing in the soul.

I stood up and leaned over to the front seat to check the dashboard, in the hope that there would be no cigarette lighter. The only endurable part of smoking as far as I was concerned was the exciting moment when the match was struck across the grit of a cardboard box or paper folder and flared into being. I hated the fusty smell of a car lighter touching the dead dry leaves and scorching the frail paper skin that contained them. No. There it was. A knob just over the pullout ashtray.

The salesman talked of a "let's-close-the-deal bonus" of summer seat covers. He had a sample of the woven strawlike material they were composed of, a cheerful red-and-white plaid.

I searched the interior of the car for a feature the man might have failed to point out to Flora. I wanted to make a contribution of some sort to the occasion.

As he showed my mother the trunk space, I squirmed around to the front seat and began to explore there.

Two women entered the showroom, spotted my mother, and one gave a shriek of recognition. It was Dot, a youngish widow from the dress shop. With her was Tansy's mother.

Through the babble that followed I understood that they were not car shopping but had dropped by to visit Dot's boyfriend, Harley, the car salesman.

The tone of the conversation immediately changed.

"Hey there, Dot," said the salesman. "Come to check out a streamlined body?"

Laughter.

"Oh, yeah," he said. "Dot here has made a study of chassis and body work, haven't you, Dot?"

Appreciation.

"And propeller shafts and universal joints?" With a leer.

Knowing glances among the women.

"Epicyclic gears? Pressure gauges? Ancillary equipment? Coupled suspension?"

Roars.

Puzzling adult merriment. Puzzling, but with a charged sort of energy that I had noticed on other occasions. Times when the simplest of happenings or words caused smiles and laughs of a category strange but alluring. I felt left out. I wanted to push my way in, to demand notice, membership in this fraternity, this secret society.

They began to calm down a bit.

I searched my mind for technical terms to add to the salesman's list. Phrases that I had heard from Randolf. One hovered on the edge of memory. What was it? Wait! I had it!

"*Reduced resistance!*" I shouted.

Total general pandemonium and collapse. Tears, sobs, the holding of sides. Tottering to lean disabled bodies against the cars for support. Slow recovery marked by individual relapse.

"In that case . . ." laughter ". . . in that case . . . I'll . . ." a gasp, a gulp of air ". . . oh, then, yes! yes!" She patted the fender of the red coupe. "In *that* case, I'll take it!" said Flora.

I had made my contribution.

To her afternoons of bridge my mother added afternoons of driving around with Dot and Tansy's mother, popping into the showroom, stopping by the country club, going to the movies in the evenings when Dot had no appointment with Harley. They began to plan, without my mother speaking to my father about it, a spring weekend at Myrtle Beach.

My mother's ventures out of town thus far had been models of decorum, to judge by her yawning returns. There was no hint of escapades.

Dot often told stories about this crowd's previous trips to South Carolina. They dwelt heavily on a character named Delia. She was a bourbon drinker, Delia, and a scamp of great renown. Last August the gang stayed at a friend's house and in the middle of the night Delia got up to go to the bathroom. She was in unfamiliar territory but was too besotted to realize it. Assuming she was at home, Delia traveled a path that should have taken her to the toilet. It took her instead to her hostess's vanity-table stool. She lifted her nightie, sat on the seat with its lavender organdy ruffle, released her burdened sphincter and, in Dot's words, "Peed like a *boss!*"

Once when Dot was over for an afternoon she glanced at her wristwatch and smacked her forehead and shouted in her deep whiskey-drinker's voice, "Oh, Christ in the bushes! Look at the time! I have a date with Harley and it's gotten so late I don't even have time to go home and change my step-ins!"

Flora and even Tansy's mother threw back their heads and hooted.

"Flora, honey, can I just call Harley and tell him to pick me up here?" Harley had been elavated from his dubious social standing by Dot's friendship.

He breezed into the house a half-hour later and, as the women rose to greet him, slid his hand under one of Dot's buttocks and gave it a heft. "Prime," he said.

He noticed I was in the room and whirled to look at me.

"Uh-oh, uh-oh," he said. "Jack Frost's wife is here." Then he turned up his coat collar and hugged his chest. Harley and I despised each other.

The shades of color for Harley's complexion had been chosen from the big Crayola selection. Sprinkled and gleaming over his body and clothing, like drops of rain when the sun breaks through, were various bits of life documentation in the form of jewelry—his high school diploma on his thick finger, Rotary Club membership in his lapel, secret society of men's fellowship on his key chain. The Baptist Adult Bible Study Class secured his tie if not his place in paradise. His black-purple iridescent socks and his shoes with pointed toes, two grackles, pecked and fed on the creatures of the oriental carpet.

"How's Mr. Simpson?" Harley asked with bravado, although I knew he would be out of the house in a flash if he heard my father's car in the driveway. "And *young* Mr. Simpson?" A glance at Flora from the side of his eyes.

"They are both well."

"I hear he's flown the coop. That's in the way of being a little subterfuge, I take it," said Harley.

"Ha ha," said Flora drily. "Honey"—to me—"go tell Sadie she can leave now. I'll drive her home in just a minute."

In the living room voices continued with Flora being firm about something to Harley.

Dot spoke. The rise at the end of her sentence indicated a question.

"I'll go," said Flora. "I'll go, but I'll take my own car."

"But that's crazy," said Dot. "You know how long that drive is? What if you have a breakdown or a flat tire?"

"No. That's what I want to do. I want to see the road in front of me and know that only *I* am going to cover it. That way it has appeal for me."

"But what if we decide to break the trip? Stay over somewhere? Or stop for a drink? There are 'wet' counties between here and Myrtle Beach. Surely you don't think Harley's going to pass those up."

"Ho no," said Harley. "Ho no. Not this boy!"

"It doesn't matter. I'll see you when you get there."

"Well, what if we bump into somebody interesting? That I know you'd like to meet?" asked Dot.

"That's not what I'm going for." Her voice changed direction. "Harley, it's *not*. What I'm going for is to put some distance between me and this town for a few days. I feel too closed in here. I can't make any decisions."

"Well, honey, contemplation is not our heavy suit. Quiet is not what we specialize in. You *know* Harley meets people a mile a minute and pulls them into the crowd. You *know* if we take on some drinking chums you'll be invited in on the fun."

"I have time to change my mind. It's not spring yet. Who knows what might happen between now and then."

"Not a lot from what I see," said Harley.

"It seems to me, Harley, that is becoming a *very* tired joke," said Flora.

"Not as tired as you must be waiting for You-Know-Who," said Harley.

I AWOKE with a start. Although I was in what I knew to be our house, objects were strangely out of proportion. I had been sleeping for some unknown reason on the living-room couch, but it was held up on a set of legs higher than the ones with which I was familiar. My eyes were on a level with the window. As I stared out the window, attempting to orient myself, I saw clouds of ice flakes in a threatening sky.

I was filled with a sense of dread, apprehension, alarm. I sensed that something corrupt, something beyond imagining was about to occur.

I slithered to the floor with the least possible movement. I crawled under the couch, but the strange furniture legs were so high that I was exposed to sight. I scrabbled along the baseboards, along the edge of the wall to the door of the room. I wanted to hide upstairs. I knew somehow that I was alone in the house. Abandoned. I made my way in torturous caught-in-quicksand moves up the stairs on all fours, crawling, each riser a hurdle, endless numbers of them.

I heard the front door open. It had not been locked!

I ran for my father's closet. I burrowed behind his clothes— his suits, his robe.

Did I hear footsteps on the stairs? No. I waited. Safe. Gone away. Safe.

Silence. I peered tentatively from behind the clothing. Nothing. I saw light coming through the high casement window of the closet wall. It was over an area of flat porch roof, easy to climb. In the corner of the window a shadow. A figure. A man.

I awoke with a start.

IT had been a rainy Saturday, the day Randolf was to leave for his new position at the mill in South Carolina.

Exhausted from my busy week of school and afternoons at the houses of my classmates, I wandered in listless but precious solitude through the house.

Randolf was long since packed, in his orderly fashion, but kept to his room doing a few last-minute tidying-up sorts of things. I heard the sound of boxes being put on a shelf, items being discarded into the wastebasket. Naked metal hangers, their clothes just removed, touched each other in tentative chings of introduction until they were swept together all in a bunch into the dark recesses of the closet.

My mother was downstairs, my father at the mill till train time, Sadie off for the weekend. I watched the rain course down the windowpanes in heavy streams. I sighed "hahhh" onto the cold glass, then wrote my name.

I wandered into my parents' room and into my mother's

closet. Far in the back she kept dresses that she no longer wore, shoes too good to be given away but that had fallen from her favor, hats that everyone had seen "a million times." I chose a brown-and-white patterned silk, tight waist with very full skirt. I had admired the way it swirled and turned when she moved. To the collar I pinned an artificial flower of deep pink. I found a hat with a veil. Heavy fuzzy dots decorated the net here and there, giving the wearer the appearance of having many beauty marks. Next, navy blue sling-heel shoes with tailored grosgrain bows. I needed gloves and a purse.

I opened her dresser drawer and found white gloves that I loved. They went up the arms to the elbow, and I thought them very grand. I took a beaded evening bag with a jeweled clasp and slithery gold chain handle, opened her compact to paint my lips.

Each time I went down a stair step, the heel of the shoe rang out and echoed through the house.

Randolf had joined my mother in the kitchen, and I teetered toward the sound of their voices.

". . . for visits, of course, but not to stay."

"It's so amazing," Flora said, "that once things *are* the way they are, they can never be changed. In so many little things you can sort of erase them, and begin again. But in life, which is the most important thing of all, whatever happens is final. There *is* no starting over. You can't say 'Wait a minute' to life. 'That wasn't what I wanted. If I had only *known* I would have wanted things another way.' "

"But that's *exactly* what I'm doing, Flora. I *am* saying 'Wait a minute' to life. It's not that I don't want the mill eventually. But I want to be self-realized first, not just directed by my father to grow and develop in his pattern."

Flora sighed. "I wasn't talking about the mill. As you must know," she said.

I wobbled into the room. She had not yet noticed I was wearing her clothes. Anxious to deflect her possible anger, I linked my arm in Randolf's. I knew that she never got mad at him.

His back had been to me and he had not even noticed my entry into the room, he was so engaged in reading Flora's face.

I gave Randolf's arm a tug and looked at him with a big, satisfied grin.

"Don't we make the perfect pair?" With sparkling eyes, I looked from one of them to the other, waiting for appreciation.

FOUR

THE child had a serious gaze. When Flora looked into its eyes it looked back unflinchingly, almost brazenly. She was sure that its eyes held knowledge of her that it could not possibly have, but there it lay, with its penetrating, steady searchlight beam. They stared at each other, she and the baby, for long periods of time, the child moving its deep blue eyes over her face. She had thought that infants possessed an unfocused wavering sort of vision, but this one's was direct and apprehending like that of a fortune teller or a seer or an oracle.

They kept the baby in their room so that they could be sure it continued to breathe through the night every night. A crib had been located in the attic, cream-colored, with sides and top of double layers of window screen. It once held Randolf. That was the one they used. It was placed in a corner of the master bedroom near the man's chest of drawers, and the baby lay looking at the glass curtains and the ever-changing patterns of light and reflected leaf shadows on them.

The man liked the baby in a distant sort of way. True, it was not a boy, but he respected it because it seemed serious and purposeful. He gave it little thought, but when he did the thought had weight.

Flora would lie at night musing and halfway listening to it breathe. On occasion it skipped in its rhythm and she was interrupted in her thoughts. It always made up for the lost beat and breathed more heavily for a time. She listened in spite of herself, and was irritated that the man in sleep was so totally free of care and oblivious to the repetitive minor emergencies of the puny living creature.

Mostly Flora was diverted by the child, but occasionally it gave her the creeps. Then she would close the double screen lid over its face and latch the hook and trip downstairs to put the radio on full force so that she couldn't hear its wails of outrage.

Flora liked the radio. It suited her that its offerings came from far away. Through air and space. It was a way of controlling distance. Of owning distance.

She turned the dial and turned it again. There was a tune she kept listening for. She couldn't remember the name. Sometimes she thought she heard it, that one certain station was playing the very song, but it always turned out to be something else. Or there would be static and, frantic with frustration, she twisted the dial and watched the needle as it passed the faint drifts of music first to one side of the station number and then the other. Furious at what had been the promise of pleasure, all but screaming with irritation, she snapped the thing off and went to walk rapidly and aimlessly in the yard. And there, through the open window, she heard the cries of the infant.

WHEN Flora was a child her father had played the fiddle. Rawlings made music—read chords from hymnbooks so old that they had shaped notations instead of round notes on the lines, and turned them into sounds. He played the foot-pedal organ in church. He drew dance reels from a harmonica. He tapped his foot and strummed a banjo. His eyes danced and his body swayed, moving inside his overalls, and she got so excited—so thrilled with the sounds and tempo and rising speech of song—that she thought she would burst. It was the purest joy she ever attained. That was when she felt complete, that was when she knew who she was.

Minnie could take it or leave it, music. It didn't call to her. The other children didn't seem to share Flora's excitement either. Their faces remained passive, their bodies didn't swell and threaten to explode.

He sang in the fields. He distracted himself from the plowing to finish a phrase. If the choice were shoving the plow deeper into a stubborn vein of clay or completing a verse nicely, he would go for the verse. His fields ripened in a ragged, haphazard way.

His reputation with the other farmers was tenuous. He didn't give his all to the land. He quit early if there was a cornhusking or a square dance for his fiddle or a revival meeting with a piano that could be pounded when the preacher paused in pounding the pulpit. Rawlings's left hand would octave up the bass, his right thrill the repentant treble. Souls would course down the aisles, fall to their knees, and all but crawl the last few steps toward Jesus. Especially the women, whose direction often tended more toward the old upright than toward the altar rail.

On Mondays, washday, they would see him and hear him, Flora and Minnie. The clothesline was behind some hedges in a sunny open spot. The hedges diverted the dust that flew up from Rawlings's plowing away from the freshly washed, damp cloth.

Minnie had a hand mangle fittted to the tub that sat in the side yard, and after she ground the wash through the rollers, as she tossed it into the basket, she sorted items in such a way that the bed linens went to the bottom, shirts were tossed to one side, dresses to the other, and undergarments on top.

Minnie took one handle of the basket and Flora took the other. They left the yard and carried it between them, each bending toward the other, each with the empty arm pulled to a curve on the outside of the body. Matching steps, they carried the load to the lines. Flora started with the undergarments. The first thing Minnie had taught her about hanging clothes was not to mix or intermingle those of the boys with those of the girls. Or even those of Minnie with those of Rawlings. When they were dry, folded and smelling of sunlight, that was the way they were carried up to the bedrooms as well. In separate stacks.

Minnie took the next row of line and began with the shirts, rapidly and expertly pinning the side tail of one to the side tail of the next so that the arms hung downward and waved in the breeze—calling, reaching for a partner.

On the third line Flora hung the pillowcases and dresser scarves and Minnie the sheets, folded exactly in half so that with their full weight pulling down the line they would not touch the ground.

Every Monday, if Rawlings was plowing nearby, he would halt Burt, remove the reins from around his own neck, tilt the plow to one side, and walk over to the clothesline to give Minnie a smacking kiss.

Flora could sense the moment of his decision to do this. Each time it was as though he had never thought of it before. The idea came to him anew each time.

He would glance over at the clothesline activity, his eyes not pausing on the small figure of Flora—he didn't even stop to identify her, she thought—and, sunstruck, squinting in the dazzle of the flapping sheets that writhed and turned in the tosses of the breeze, he followed some memory of nighttime sheets that called him from the plow.

He stepped over furrows, stones, clumps of tall grass up-rooted, and made his way to Minnie, growing taller and taller, diminishing Minnie as he approached so that he had to bend to kiss the person who had, a moment before, seemed so towering a presence to Flora.

On days that the clotheslines were bare she looked at the empty lengths of wire. They imprinted on her mind and caused her to think of the spans of wire along the sides of the country roads. She didn't know if they were telephone wires or electric or even telegraph. In any case, none came to the farmhouse.

The creosoted poles had been cut down in the piney woods of South Carolina where they grew, she had heard—miles and miles of them—in turpentine, incendiary forests. One spark and half a county flared.

The arms of the poles bore fingers of green-bubbled glass spirals, ringed about with buzzing, snapping cables. Transformer boxes hummed and clicked with secret messages, conspiracies of travel and intrigue. What lives there must be in some places on this earth.

Sometimes the spans of wire marked a distant road where she hadn't even known there was one. You could find your way by them, she thought. They drew maps in the air.

She looked at the wires stretching for miles. She looked at the sunlight on the flat open fields. Even if you didn't stare at the sky, she found, you could see the clouds as they passed over on their way somewhere else, as they cast shadows on the rows of cotton or potatoes.

Lettuce rested quietly on the earth, its roots barely holding the soil. The silk of the corn waved and pointed away. The wheat leaned and yearned. The animals, if not fenced and penned, wandered. Roamed. If not chained and hobbled, lost all sense of belonging and disappeared. Seeds blew on the breezes, dust rose and traveled, rivers passed you by, flowed on away.

SHE was most free to look at the boy with impunity at meals. As the lady of the house, the hostess, she could observe his hands, his face, pass the salt and touch him, lean over his shoulder to pour tea. His hands were golden, smooth, the fingers beautifully articulated; fair gleams indicated tufts of blondness. When he handled objects he closed his fingers around them as though it were the first time in the universe that man had opposed his thumb to his forefinger. The progress of royalty into court could not have been more grand than his lifting of a water glass.

His eyes were so clear it was like flying to look into them. Each time she did she felt the wrench when she landed on earth again. She poised, waiting for the next chance. Answer me, answer me, she thought. The little girl spilled milk and Flora rushed to pat Randolf's spattered shirt with a damp towel. Nothing.

The man talked of politics, of the war in China, the turmoil in Europe.

The boy talked of tennis, of the coach who had turned the university team into winners, of his own efforts in matches and sets.

She remembered country games of horseshoes, softball. How, when she made a hit, she dug her bare toes into the powdery dust of the school lot and pumped her way around the bases, new breasts bouncing, skirt tangling between her legs, the familiar summer smell of girl sweat on her forehead, her lip, under her arms. Thumbs alternately rising and pointing to her flaming cheeks as she made, fists clenched, for base, with all her heart for home.

Outbursts of the man's explosive temper the boy dealt with as though he were in the presence of utmost reason, answering the words and content and not dealing with the tone of the voice, the sarcasm. And within minutes the man was talking sense, speaking quietly, with pauses and moments of reflection.

Whereas she and the man argued bitterly. He shouted, she became affronted, wounded, fled trembling with loathing from his presence.

The boy made her feel things she had never felt before, have longings she barely understood. She wanted to touch him in places that bewildered her, do things with him that she had never dreamed people could want to do. He excited and stupefied her. She came to understand what bodies were for. Why they were of value. What instruments they could become. How they could be loved, longed for. How it could be agony to be parted. But most of all she understood what she had done to herself. What she had lost, what she had given away, given up, without knowing, unaware.

THE scenery of Flora's dreams was still set with items from her childhood. The round-bottomed metal dishpan, the flatirons heating on the cookstove, the mirror–flecked, wavering glass–hung on a high nail, loop of wire visible. The old bedspreads and quilts, the door-ajar wardrobe, the pegs on the back porch where the winter barn-cleaning coats hung, too soiled to be stored in Minnie's house. The cast-iron syrup kettle, the long-handled waffle iron, the tin water dipper shaped like the constellation. Wall calendars from the cotton gin or the flour mill. The pale flowers and ornate lettering of Minnie's childhood embroidery–"Home, Sweet Home"–that hung on the shelf above Rawlings's fiddle case.

They ate and they were clean, but Minnie couldn't take them much further than that. The girls' hair was bound in pigtails so tight that their faces wore a look of perpetual incredulity. The boys wore overalls with no shirts, the denim bibs stood out stiffly showing boy flesh and the thin upper arms of fast growers. At times the heat of the sun grew so fierce that the metal fasteners of the garments seared the bare skin they touched. The family wore straw hats when they worked the fields, Rawlings's more sweat-stained than the boys'. Even Burt, the mule, had a hat, an old one of Rawlings's, with places cut out for his ears. He appreciated it.

Flora's favorite time on the farm was when the potatoes were ready to be turned out of their bed of earth. The same plow that had covered the red soil over their eyes, putting them in the dark, now, digging deeper and to the side, revealed the reproductions of their night. Picking up the potatoes was one of the first field jobs that a small child could handle. The children piled the tubers in rows. Minnie and the boys dropped them into burlap sacks that they dragged along behind them.

Some potatoes the plow split, and the white flesh shone wet, the thin tan skin sliced away as though with a kitchen knife. She felt bad about those. They healed over with a scab and never looked right again. As you worked you were told to brush the dirt aside to search under the furrow for those that the plow might have missed. The worms had been busy in the night of earth, too, so sometimes she pulled up a squirming rotten hive of slugs that collapsed to a viscous stink in her hand. Or she tenaciously dug, nails bending back over the quick, only to turn up a stone the color and shape of a fine spud.

But she was in the fields with Rawlings. She was part of things, valuable. Out of the eight daughters, she was determined to be the one he would think about. The best one.

Sometimes they ate rabbits, squirrels, possums. The boys hunted, hounds at their sides, under their control–dignified working dogs who knew their jobs and liked them. The dogs pointed, muscular bodies quivering inside loose skin, to bird or furred creature, recognized the names of prey. "We're goin' for rabbit, girl, git me a rabbit." The boys skinned the small body, revealing the red-blue flesh of the kill, clumps of fur sticking to their hands, bits of bloodied fur clinging to their clothes, wiping the knife after, tossing the hide to the dogs, who sniffed it, tore it, played with it, when it was old rolled in it, perfuming their bodies with the afterglow of putrefaction. Occasionally when some marking or pattern of the fur caught the fancy of one boy he scraped it, dried it, stretched it and used the hide as decoration on his wall over his bed or on the door to the room.

Blain, the older brother, didn't like possums, their thyroid eyes, their fingered hands, their hissing. They looked like they knew too much. Possums, though gluey to his taste, were larger than squirrel; you only needed one of them to make a stew, but its upside-down hanging white face gave him the willies. He tried to back out of hunting possums with neither Rawlings nor his brother finding out why.

They ate persimmon pie, carefully waiting for the orange fruit to ripen to pulp-soft so that it wouldn't swell their mouths closed. Picked blackberries, becoming in the process part of the food chain themselves as the chiggers burrowed under their skin. Fished in the branches and brooks, went for perch and catfish when they got as far as the lake.

There had been summer days when she was just a little thing, when Minnie had put her to washing dishes, needing her help even as she left the cradle, pushed out by the next one. Minnie made it into almost a game. She still had the patience then for mildness. She carried the bench from the back porch and set it in the sun out in the workyard, laid on it a dish towel or two, and then gave Flora the old metal dishpan with warm water and soap, a soft rag, another pan with clear rinse water, and let her wash the cups and saucers, slowly, at a child's contemplative pace . . . bubbles rising and popping, plates and forks rubbed and rubbed in the sun of a summer afternoon . . . rag doll nearby, its stitched eyes alert, birds calling, leaves moving softly, a whinny from Burt, the low of a cow from over in the pasture.

Then the call, "Whooo, Min," and off her mother went, stomach before her, hands pressing the small of her back as she followed his call, walked out to listen to his questions.

Minnie kept the chickens. Rawlings kept the bees, dressing, when they swarmed, in layers and layers of clothing to dull the stings, searching frantically each new time for his heavily veiled hat. "Minnie! Whooo, Min! Where's the gol-darned hat? Oh, my. Oh, my Lord. Them gosh-derned bees is aswarmin'."

And each time after the swarming, Flora meant to watch him, to follow him, to observe his throwing aside of the hat he kept meaning to repair and improve. To bring it to him in a quiet moment, to work on. But as he pulled out the stings that penetrated the veils and wads of cloth, as she saw his face and body lump and swell, she forgot. She wanted to be praised, noticed, singled out as the one who helped him, but each time she forgot to watch his careless casting away of an item he would surely need again.

There was the flurry to robe him, tie the ankles of his pants tight to his boots, fit his padded gloves over the wrists, arrange the weighted net of the hat, and when he was dressed, grown more huge, more tall, he was an awesome sight. A different person, like some god of old, biblical, deflecting arrows, striding into battle holding a smoking torch to stupefy the enemy, the humming armies of Armageddon. They watched from the window as he walked into a hurricane of bees, their nervous excitement changed to rage, their furry bodies and insect legs clotting to him, crawling over each other in their fury, bees between his fingers, diving for his eyes, seeking the vulnerable rent in his armor, rising, circling, then landing on his body again and again. They stabbed and died, stabbed and died, falling from the body of a giant, tramped under his feet at the end as he carried, dripping in his hands, their gold, their treasure, even, even, their queen.

ONCE the man took the boy out of town with him on a brief business trip. To give him the experience of dealing with distributors, salesmen. To introduce him to people he would write to or telephone in future days.

They left early in the morning. Flora returned to the house after seeing them to the car in her wrapper and called a bewildered Sadie, giving her the day off.

When the child cried she pressed bits of toast or apple into its waving fist as it sat all day in the crib.

Flora climbed the steps to stare, hands cupped around her eyes, through the panes of the locked door to Randolf's attic garage room. Order.

She wandered in the yard in her robe, picking up a seed pod, a shiny stone, the broken transparent wings of an insect. She sat for some hours in the dusty cobwebbed attic of the house. When it grew dark she found herself stirring oatmeal for the child with a smooth twig.

She drew the shades in Randolf's bedroom and searched his closet, his dresser, under his bed, his bookshelves, his desk. Nothing said "Flora."

She took off her robe and lay down on his bed. But nothing here said that she was in his thoughts.

The travelers had returned in two days, the boy's business acumen confirmed, the man content.

Over the long months, over time, what she and the man did she kept in some other compartment of her mind. It didn't impinge on what she thought of as her real life. As she learned how to enjoy sex, to unlock the secrets of satisfaction, she began in the night to give voice to her moments of release. She expected the man to quiet her. To put his hand over her mouth, even. And in the light of day explain to her that it was not right for the boy to hear such sounds. But he never did. Either he was overcome himself and didn't hear them as real sounds or he thought of them as being muffled by the dark of night. What was not exposed to the light of day did not exist.

She thought the boy would become aroused, eager, close to the act. She was drawing him in.

One night when the man sank into the sedated state of completion, she got up and left their room. She closed the door, leaving the man and child breathing steadily.

She thought she might have heard another door click.

She walked down the hall to the empty bedroom next to Randolf's, lay on top of the bed, thighs still moist, and listened for sounds of restlessness. Messages from one who waits.

THEY came for her in the middle of the night. She awoke to find their hands on her, in the dark, pulling her from the bed. She would have cried out, but then the other children in the long narrow room would have awakened and have known they were taking her. It was her shameful secret. The ones they sent to get her were hairy, loathsome creatures, and at first she thought they were the ones who would do it.

They carried her to some underground place where the doctors were waiting.

"You want to have babies when you grow up, don't you?" they asked as they placed her on the table. She nodded. "Then this is what must happen. We are only going to find out if you can have babies."

They began to inspect her, sometimes only outside and sometimes very far in. They touched places, probing, looking, discussing.

A group of old men huddled together in a corner of the room at the edge of the dim light until they were driven away, out the door. But even after they left they formed an excited group and peeked through a crack in the wall to watch. From time to time one of them would escape the eye of the guard and scuttle into the room to wet a finger in her or pass a hand over her chest and then be dragged, giggling and scuffling, away again.

They brought in a young man, handsome, naked, and put him beside her and told him what to do to her. And although they were evil doctors, she was relieved when she was reassured that they really only needed to do this to see if she could have babies when she grew up.

The young man was touching her, lightly, brushingly, the way they told him to, she was in a bed now, in a room that might have been home—the old rocking chair looked familiar for a minute and then changed and didn't, worn rag rug, caged, listless bird, in the air a faint trace of yeast bread rising—and the young man was touching her, lightly, brushingly, her eyes glazed and focused far away, her thoughts saying *at last at last*, then, at the foot of the bed a dark movement, something sinister—a shape— she tried to pull away, tried to leave the bed, tried to flee, but could not stir, and a grizzle-faced man rose from the covers and with a sly grin, held back the covers from his nakedness. "Now I get you," he said, and the young man was gone, "you've come to the wrong house and now I get you," smiling evil, "and I'm going to teach you what you have to do. I'm going to show you the things you have to do, and you have to do them over and over, I get to decide what they are," he smiled, "it's to punish you," evil, "and I'm ready to begin. I'm not going to wait for you to grow up. I'm ready to begin. I'll do whatever I want," and he smiled, "whatever I want," and the group of old men scuttled in again to help hold her.

TOWARD dawn she heard the click of the back door and the almost silent steps of the boy as he climbed the stairs and reentered his room. He came to the breakfast table on time and with an impassive face.

The boy left for classes. As the man returned to the master bedroom for his watch and keys, Flora ran out the back door, across the yard and up the slat stairs to peer through the door-glass into the garage room.

It was a shambles. Books and tools on the floor. Pictures torn from the walls. His tennis racket, its frame broken, the strings cut from top to bottom with one sharp stroke.

The almost tender smile remained on her face as she came back to the house, to the front hall, and looked up at the man as he descended the stairs.

He stopped when he reached her.

"Today," he said, as he put on his hat, turning it first a time or two in his hands, "today, I want you to move the child. Move the baby out of our room."

FIVE

THE waitresses in the local café set the men up for the day. Even if an individual had consumed two fried eggs, bacon, grits, biscuits, and coffee at home, before work he went straight over to Hull's by the depot for another cup of coffee and a general bucking up from the women in white. The women's greetings were democratic, the same for community leaders as for the little guy. But the big-mouthed flirts with their outrageous protestations of love—those men who loudly and publicly proclaimed undying devotion to Gussie or Peg or to fat Lolla—were the true favorites. The café was ripe with smoke and camaraderie, the swagger of the male population as it girded for another day of the earned wage.

The town shoeshine stand was set up just outside the barbershop and kept two black men going—smiling, calling to customers, slapping cloth and wielding brushes all morning. When they really got moving, brushes flying on alternate sides of the polish-laden shoe, a man had to concentrate to hold his foot steady on the pedestal. Only the old-timers, men who had enjoyed comfortable incomes for years, had mastered reading their newspapers during a shine. Others held papers up and just pretended to move their eyes over the rippling print.

When the streets cleared of men—when they entered their

stores, their banks, their offices—women began to arrive. Earliest to be seen were the stout matrons, heavy of breast, sturdy of shoe, wearing hats and gripping serious handbags with thick handles and good, secure snap closings. Carried in each handbag for further reference and folded with razor-sharp precision was the bulletin from last Sunday's church service.

These women, in a town safe and free of crime, feared pilferage, and when the seasons changed, they shopped for the obligatory new handbag with ferocity. As they stood in the shops trying the snaps of first one bag and then another, the sound was of a city under siege, scattered street fighting breaking out here and there in some beleaguered quarter. They looked for the purse with a closing that could take off an intruding hand at the wrist.

Later the ladies of a higher social strata drove in stately rows down Main Street, motoring with gloved hands, to park, nose in, at the curb. They peered over the giant steering wheels, brows creased, straining to see through the windshields even in finest weather, as though caught in impenetrable fog. They understood that driving was a serious discipline—one of the male religions, actually—and if they were to be nuns in the order, they must exert great energies and concentration. As adherents, to prove their worthiness, they made constant small adjustments of the steering wheel—"steering" being synonymous with "driving"—so that on wet days the puffy tires left zigzag patterns on the pavement. The cars, like patient oxen, maneuvered their wide bellies and slow feet into place and, with impeccable good manners, overlooked the surfeit of command.

There was on the front page of the local newspaper a brief column, "Along the Boulevard." It was the first item glanced at after the headlines by all the ladies who had that morning paraded the streets. They looked to see if their progress had been noted. My mother always laughed when she read it.

"Look at these corkers," she said. "You'd think this was New York or Chicago or something. How can they call this 'news'?"

But when she first made it into print—"Pretty Mrs. Flora Simpson spotted in her fine new bonnet"—I noticed that she clipped the item and put it in a drawer and went back to it over and over. There was one about Randolf a month or so later. "Randolf Simpson with his ever-present tennis racket." She clipped that one, too.

My father and his fishing friend, Gabe, had a falling-out. It was over some business advice my father gave.

Gabe was in real estate and wanted to develop a considerable parcel of land out near the country club. He wanted people to buy two-acre lots and put up big expensive houses. He had managed to acquire a good deal of acreage and had been spreading the word that the location was the upcoming place to build the finest residences. Several families had already built there, and once the women began saying that they loved it, that no, they didn't feel isolated away from downtown and so on, interest mounted.

The unimproved property was no trouble, it was just a matter of clearing the brush and cutting a few trees so that prospective buyers could see the lay of the land. But here and there, mostly out along the road, were the modest homes of people who had lived in the area for years, from before the country club was built. Several eyesores Gabe had no problem buying and tearing down. Other houses were neat and well kept and they gave him no concern either.

There was one place, however, that really had him stumped. It was close to the road and had to be passed on the way to two of the best, most beautifully situated parcels. Gabe could just *see* huge white brick houses, columns out front, glossy vines growing up the several chimneys. He could all but *hear* the crunch of gravel as expensive cars passed between rhododendron and laurel to pull up before grand porches and doors. His mouth watered when he thought of the real-estate values in that neighborhood in the years to come: other lots, the resale of houses, then shops, stores, a universe of deals revealed itself, played out in the deeds and leases of his mind.

"The fly in the ointment," he told my father, "is old man Huggins. His house is not bad, looks presentable. But there's that damn pile of junk in his front yard. That pile of junk has been there for years. God-awful mess. Old tires, crushed fenders, ironing boards, rags, I don't know what all. I can't figure out why the hell it's there or how to get him to move it. If I could sell the lots first and then push through the two-acre zoning, I could get the police to give him a summons to move the stuff. But until I close on the lots I can't get the zoning. He won't sell me his house either, sly old son of a bitch. Won't even name a price."

"Don't bother with the house," said my father. "Just buy the trash. Send somebody around who claims to be a junk dealer. Happening to pass through town with an empty truck. Have him make Huggins a small offer. Don't go yourself or he'll be on to it. Send somebody else."

Gabe did. The pile of junk was turned over to the mystery buyer, loaded on his truck, and carted to the dump.

Gabe was jubilant.

But before he could complete a deal on the lots a new pile of junk appeared. Again he sent somebody around to buy it. Again it was hauled to the dump. Yet another pile appeared, bigger, older, and rustier than before.

"Christ, Simpson," said Gabe. "I want to thank you for your sound advice."

"Who'd you send around to buy it?" my father asked.

"Like you said, I didn't go myself. Didn't even send one of the boys from the office. They've all been seen over there measuring lots and driving stakes. But I didn't want to lay out big money just to have a pile of junk hauled. Most fellows would charge you a dollar for that kind of work. Driving, loading, dumping. I thought I was being smart," he said defensively. "I hired one of the ole boys who hangs around outside the poolroom. Got the whole thing done for fifty cents."

"The poolroom! Who?"

"I got ole Beer-boy Blanton. Took that stumblebum all afternoon but I got the whole thing done for only fifty cents."

"Gabe, you are a goddamned idiot. Any fool can spot Beer-boy for a shill. A five-year-old *child* could spot Beer-boy. You can write off those two lots. You might just as well forget them right now. Either that or you're going to be buying junk, more and more expensive junk, solid-gold junk, till hell freezes over."

So my father didn't think he would be going fishing as often come spring.

On a winter day of brilliant blue I asked, "Won't you miss the fishing?"

He sat, the newspaper by his side, one leg folded in right-angled man-fashion, knee out, and laid across the other.

"I like feeling the weight of the line," he said. "Choosing the leader. I like the places, Fontana Dam, the reservoir, the Dan River, Dudley Shoals. I like the vegetation. I like staying away longer than we should for the evening rise. I never tire of fishing. It's a reliable pleasure. But Gabe feels foolish for letting me know the price of his kingdom. Men don't want you to know the price of their kingdom. And Gabe decided that his was only worth fifty cents.

"You see," he went on, "it was clear to old man Huggins—because Beer-boy is such a bum—that somebody wanted the junk out of the way. Not that somebody wanted the *junk*. Now old man Huggins' kingdom is spite. If he thought somebody was interested in junk, he would have taken his time collecting another pile, to spite the junk dealer. He was willing, even though he's poor, to pay the price of *not* getting paid in coin. The spite made it more valuable than money. And while he was taking his time collecting junk for another pile, Gabe could have sold the lots. But Huggins hurried to build up another pile to spite whoever it was who wanted *no* junk."

He lit a cigarette.

"Now, I gave Gabe some advice. That's risky. People don't

always act on your advice the way you think is logical. The way you would act yourself. And many times the way they act has to do with the price of their kingdom. When you give advice you very often end up needing some yourself." He laughed ruefully.

"Now when spring comes, I will probably find that giving Gabe advice has spoiled my fishing pleasure for a while.

"I like looking at the water, studying the currents. I watch it flow, catch the light. I figure out the patterns the fish use in feeding, when they slow and turn, where they dart and hurry. *They* have a kingdom. A perfect place. I like to spot an old warrior, the old browns mostly, one who's been stung and scarred and who ought to know about the hook. I keep looking for one who won't take the bait. When I spot one like that I go there again and again. Use all my skill to catch him. But at the same time I hope he'll fool me—not rise to the bait, not risk his kingdom for something bright and shiny. That he'll know what's false. A big old-timer. Those are the ones I go for. To find out what their kingdom is worth."

"If you know you'll miss the fishing, why won't you go alone? Or just with Judson?"

"Well, I could. And I might if Gabe doesn't get over his sulk. But I'll wait a while first. So that he sees that we miss him. Anyway, it gives the game warden a rest." He smiled and picked up his paper.

HE stands out on the country road, my father. He leans against the side of his car, round-brimmed hat pushed back from his forehead, and smokes a cigarette. He listens to the birdcalls, watches a hawk, smells the fresh-ground-pepper smell of deep woods, the dampness of water running over stone, the heady opiate of pine needles.

It is winter now but soon it will be daytime forever; soon the arms of the trees on distant mountaintops will toss the sunlight back into the sky.

He visits the hatchery, observes the fingerlings in their shallow rectangular nursery, dips the long-handled seine into the school to watch the babies panic, hop and escape. He moves to another trough and looks for a long time at the handsome adolescents, as they make their endless, circling turns, their rainbows enchanting each other, over and over again, ever anew.

I WONDERED about fish rising to the bait and how many times a day they did that. How many bugs did it take to satisfy the hunger of a fish? The measurement of the amount of nourishment required by the lower forms of life—rodents, insects, pests, vermin—perplexed me.

Would or would not a green pea be a sufficient meal for a mouse? Half a meal? Or half left over?

How could a bee possibly sip honey all day and not burst? I understood that they took some home to the hive, but how much? Just a little or all afternoon's worth?

I liked picture books of the sort that showed the father mouse carrying home on his shoulder a grape, and then the next sequence where the family gathered around the table and the father carved the grape, watermelon fashion, with a miniature carving knife. But I understood that these were not realistic or scientific.

And why was man the only creature that did not spend the entire day seeking sustenance? Surely it was what we were meant to do. Feeding, picking through bushes, ripping up roots from the soil and even popping squirming things into our mouths.

> See the pretty pansies
> Growing in a row.
> Pick the pretty pansies
> To make more pansies grow.

That was the sort of lesson printed in our "science" book, a book carefully chosen to endanger no fundamentalist religious concepts. This book had no relationship to the realities of nature as I perceived them.

I often found similarities in the physical forms of natural things. Ideas were used over and over. I could see that God, the Great Architect, had had a few favorite creative thoughts, using them, storing them away for a while, and then pulling them out and using them again, just like my mother with her sewing patterns. He made minor modifications in buttons (nipples) or adaptations for land or water wear (skin, scales) but He did not come up with endless new geometric or organic models. And as for each snowflake being unique, as we were assured they were by the schoolteacher, and, for some reason, by the preacher time and again, why bother if all the flakes did was melt when they hit the sidewalk, or adhere to each other if it was freezing? The snowflake caper told a little more about God's perversity than it did about His originality, I thought.

Once I had seen pictures of squid and thought them absolutely unique. One of a kind. I was disappointed to find them planted in our garden the next spring by Alexander and now called "asparagus roots." The squid of earth. Imprisoned. Forced to swim in the slow motion of cell growth in the thick dark medium of soil.

That waving puff of fragrant delight, the mimosa blossom, was spun from the same thin thread as corn silk. Before a squash flower became a flower it was a tiny green penis. Half a pecan—larger and covered with hair, but the same red-brown folds and convolutions—was my mother's genital area glimpsed through her parted robe.

Our science books were given to us to protect us from the idea of Darwinism, to defend us from the festering mind of a Scopes. But if God had used the same physical forms in an economy of creative thought, why then should it startle that He might do the same with brains? Why *not* spring the mind of man from an ape. It was just like Him. It was in character, it certainly seemed to me. God copycatted Himself. How could a thinking person doubt it? How could that next logical step be denied in the face of a repetitive natural world? God had His limits.

THE apes. The great apes. Flying through trees, swinging on twisted, braided vines, spilling, tumbling past parrots and orchids, looping through vast twilit places, leaf-patterned, frond-brushed.

Animals enraptured with the idea of mother love. Enfolding, enveloping their babies. Given arms of extra length to enclose, to embrace their babies. All day the baby clutches tufts of mother fur with its spatulate fingers, perfect half-moon nails, and wraps its bowed, bony legs around her hips, her pelvic saddle, feels her draw breath with the curling instep of its infant foot. All day the mother ape lazily swings, moving with first one long furred arm and then the other, from dappled sun to cooling shade, finding berries for the baby's pushing lips, fruit for its fist.

The side of the baby's face, its cheek, is laid against the flat leather breast of the mother, its ear hears the pounding exertion of her flying heart as they swing past parrot and orchid, past insect and toucan, past all the splendors of tropical life.

And at night the mother strips branches and boughs to make a nest for the two of them. Together, before they close the lids over their thoughtful brown eyes, they search the scraps of visible sky for stars, for moon, for planets. Then together they sleep in the warmth of fur and shelter. The grave, elderly face of the baby stretches in a smile. And the mother holds the baby in her arms. And holds it. All night long the mother holds the baby to her heart.

MINNIE died. She had a fire going in the cookstove, country ham sizzling in the pan. She turned to Rawlings from her breadboard, a look of amazement on her face, to see if he felt the reverberations from the astounding thing that had happened in her chest. Rawlings reached for her as she fell. He lifted her but he had trouble seeing her. He continued to see instead the white scraps of dough on the flour-dusted table. They showed an outline where each perfect circle of biscuit had been removed.

He cut her corset strings with the butcher knife but it didn't help.

He rose, then, in the mornings from the vast strange flatness of their bed. He traveled at night, ill equipped, poorly outfitted, impressed to serve on a voyage not of his choosing. Bewildered, he made it through the days with his knees slightly bent, his hands surprising him—two unknowns who insisted on accompanying him here and there, begging for recognition and to be his friends.

Since he couldn't lose his grief, he released his mind instead and forgot the way to the barn, stood poised between stove and table, plate growing cold in his grasp. Word came back to Flora that he chased and fumbled with the widow ladies of his church, wearing on his face the silly, leering grin of a hick.

"THERE'S the mill, of course," I heard my father say. "And the warehouse and the office building. The houses. The farms. The insurance and the cars. This house and all its furnishings.

"The things that were Nettie's should be offered to Randolf. And I'll leave him the director's seat on the board. You and Randolf will share the profits of the mill equally while you remain the owners and divide the price you get if it's eventually sold.

"You and Randolf will share only the mill. I'll leave everything else to you. I think a man should have to work his way up in the world. Then it's *his* work that he values. It's *his* work that he owns. It doesn't do to leave a man too much. Randolf is the goods. He'll move right up, come right along by himself. I'm confident of that.

"You'll look out for the child from your share."

They sat in the living room on winter evenings in the glow of the fire, their voices subdued and low as he murmured night after night what she would have when he was gone.

He described to her the caution she must exercise in dealing with lawyers and real-estate people and tenants. He trusted the present mill staff, he told her. After all, their welfare was involved in the successful running of the business, along with hers. He did not feel them to be cheats, and in any case, Randolf would be there to oversee.

Her answers were thoughtful, perceptive, mature. Her voice took on a new quality at these times. He would set her a hypothetical problem or ask her a complex question, and I could tell that most of the time her answer satisfied him.

In the daytimes a difference in her bearing was discernible. A force and confidence I hadn't noticed before.

He spoke of wills and deeds. Titles and taxes and executors. He gave cautions on sales and profits, advice on percentages and distributions. There were leases and liens, notes coming due, stocks, bonds, trusts.

His voice came from a great depth, from deep in his being, as though he were already withdrawn, already set away, launched into a lonesome distance. Night after winter night he spoke of the same things. His was the song of a mighty whale reverberating from untold leagues, calling, listening to his own watery echo through the green salt darkness. His sound traveled the great circle course, navigated through the currents, eddies, the vagaries of drift, avoided false headings, snares for the unwary. The song called, coaxed, enchanted.

"And if I'm sick, if I'm more dead than alive, if my mind is gone, if there is no hope and I'm in pain, don't let them keep me alive. I don't want to think about lying in a hospital, moaning and gasping for breath for weeks or months on end. Don't let them do that to me. Don't let them hook me up to air machines or lung machines or inject me with drugs to speed up my blood or run tubes into me or beat with their fists on my heart."

He didn't know what it was Flora wanted, but he knew it was something he had been unable to give her. He felt her dissatisfaction even through their lovemaking, even though he knew he satisfied her physically. He thought about it and worked on it and decided on a course of action, a wooing, a declaration of love in his own style, naming his own offering. And the offering wasn't the deeds or the property or the mill or the house. He was offering his death to Flora. He was promising to die. My father was naming the price of his kingdom.

EASTER was to arrive early that year, in March, and we expected Randolf's next visit for that holiday. My father was surprised when he wrote to announce that he wanted to come for a weekend in February instead. Randolf enclosed a note to Flora asking if he might bring a houseguest.

I thought Adelaide was wonderful. She had blond hair and round red cheeks and the most engaging giggle I ever heard. Most girlish giggles are forced, practiced semishrieks, grating to hear and produced from a shallow region of the mind that has absorbed the concept that the giggle is endearing but has not taken notice that it must be genuine. Adelaide's giggle came to her all unexpected and was a celebration, a cavorting essence of breath that said, "I am a girl and you are a boy and we are alive and you delight me." She said it to Randolf over and over again, effortlessly and bubblingly, with pure joy and surprise at its arrival.

Randolf and I showed Adelaide to her room. He carried her bag, placed it on the folding luggage rack, then turned and went immediately to stand just outside her door.

"I'll stop by for you in a quarter of an hour," he said and left.

Adelaide invited me in to watch her unpack.

The first thing she did was to take from her suitcase—where it had been wrapped in tissue paper and placed on top of her folded clothes—a stuffed toy, a penguin. It wore a top hat and a jaunty bow tie. She kissed it and propped it against the pillows on the bed. I instantly determined never to travel without a stuffed toy when I got to be as old as Adelaide.

She removed and hung up the jacket of her traveling suit. Her outfit had caught Flora's eye and immediately put her off-balance, I thought, because the lining of Adelaide's jacket was of the same patterned silk as her blouse, a fashion possibility that had never occurred to Flora.

I watched Adelaide's hands as she hung and smoothed garments. They were slender and tan and, I thought, of transcending beauty.

After the performance (three acts: Clothes Viewing, Cosmetics Arranging, Shoe Lining-Up) I went to my room, giddy. I examined my hands. Scant potential. I closed my eyes tight and pressed my lips together. I began at that moment a new daily regimen of willing my hands to grow up to be just like Adelaide's.

ADELAIDE played tennis, and she and Randolf talked about the winning team at the university and the coach and what a terrific job he was doing.

Flora got agitated when they talked of things she knew nothing about. We all sat in the sunroom watching, through the banks of windows, the dusty drift and fall of snow. As the talk moved from one topic to another, Flora assessed Adelaide, watched her gestures, the turns of her head, the sparkle that lay in the upswept curve of her lashes.

Adelaide had a freedom about her, an honesty of attention to what people said, an appealing openness that Flora attempted to counter with a surly sort of smoldering emotion. Randolf was alert to Flora's state and went out of his way to placate her by directing his questions to her and giving weight to her answers.

Adelaide lived in South Carolina in the town where Randolf

worked. He was continuing his college courses in that town at night and Adelaide was a boarding student at a women's college some distance away. They saw each other only on holidays. They looked forward to spending time together over the summer, they said, when Adelaide would be at home.

Flora tried to persuade them to stay with us during Randolf's mill vacation. In our town. In our house. She offered all sorts of inducements.

"I could give you lifts to the country club," she said. "I could drive you to the courts."

"That's thoughtful of you, Flora. Thank you," said Randolf. "We have decided, though, that wherever we are, we'll ride bicycles to the courts. It strengthens the leg muscles."

"What about when it rains? Sometimes there are terrible showers, what about then?"

"Well, of course, when it rains we don't play tennis. The moisture causes the strings to relax."

I could tell Flora didn't share my delight with Adelaide. She hugged her just the way she did Dot and Trudy but she treated her like a little girl at the same time. Flora got edgy and shrill if I mentioned Adelaide when we were another room. She made funny little remarks that I didn't understand. In fact, she began to seem irritated with Randolf himself, the only person she invariably had patience for in the past.

Adelaide came from an old and distinguished South Carolina family. She was modest and circumspect, and when she was home from school was hovered over by her family. She had been permitted to visit us only because she and Randolf traveled with her aunt and uncle who were paying a visit elsewhere in town.

I watched them closely to see if they were "in love," a condition that was beginning to intrigue me. If any scrap of conversation edged too closely toward the idea of physical contact, both Adelaide and Randolf grew lines between their brows and got quiet. There was no touching between them. They were comradely. I decided they truly liked each other and were moving at a pace comfortable to them toward the exalted state of being "sweethearts." I also felt that Adelaide was moving toward that state faster than Randolf was. She was ready for a sign. I knew men to be plodding as they approached love, to drag their feet, and slant straight backward like characters in an animated cartoon, digging their heels into the ground so that sprays of soil and pebbles flew up on both sides while they shouted, "No, no! I'm all right the way I am. Alone! Do you hear me? Help! Help!"

As closely as I watched them, and it was constant, there was another who, without looking or seeming to, watched them more astutely, more narrowly, more unceasingly than I.

THERE were goblets for water, linen napkins, candles in the middle of the table, and my mother had been to the florist for a bunch of flowers. Adelaide laid the silverware and I did the chair arranging, placing the front legs of each chair precisely, so as to match the design on the rug beneath it. My father and Randolf were sitting in the living room in front of the fire and talking. Flora was in the kitchen heating up the food that Sadie had fussed over for days. We were eating late on Sunday evening, and I had school the next day. I was to go straight to bed after dessert.

Flora for the whole weekend had been more attentive to my father than usual. She flustered over him when he went outdoors, telling him to wear his muffler, his gloves; she made much over him at dinner, asking what size serving he wanted, keeping his coffee cup filled. The four grown-ups made two pairs, although it didn't come out exactly even; since my father was so many years older than the others, there was some left over.

The dinner progressed in the usual way of grown-up meals, slowly. The chicken, the gravy, the dumplings, the sweet potatoes, the peas, the baked apples, the pickled peaches, the salad, the biscuits, finally the pies. Then coffee.

I became groggy. I worried about getting enough sleep. Sometimes the teacher made everyone tell what foods they had had for breakfast and how many hours' sleep they had had the night before. To teach good health habits. It was unthinkable to lie. I would say we had had company, I decided. That lent a certain cachet.

HE had taken me aside in the late morning while everyone else was out walking in the light snow that flurried and stopped, flurried and stopped.

"I want you to keep a secret," he said. "I have to know if you can keep a secret for me."

"Yes," I said. "I can."

"I want you to give her this." He was holding a squarish white envelope in his hand. "Sometime today. In a private moment. I want you to be the mailman."

He parted the opening of the unsealed envelope and showed me a corner of the message inside.

"And you mustn't tell who sent it."

I studied his face to see if he were joking. It seemed unlike him to be serious about the kind of thing he ordinarily scorned as frivolous. He was embarrassed by the notion, I decided, but determined to carry it through anyway. He was sincere.

I loved the whole idea.

"I promise. I won't ever tell her who gave it to me. I won't tell who sent it."

"All right, thank you. A private moment. Remember."

THE pauses in the conversation grew longer. They had done nothing all weekend but talk. At last they had run out of topics. I hoped they would push back their chairs and scatter from the table so I would have a chance to deliver the letter. I forced myself to keep my eyes open.

"Oh, I'm so full and cozy," said Adelaide. "I dread the thought of that long trip."

"I don't see how anybody could dread a trip," said Flora with an edge to her voice. "I haven't been anywhere for as long as I can remember. I would welcome a trip." She glanced at Randolf. "I would *love* to take a trip."

It occurred to me that if Flora continued, Adelaide might be in for a few rough moments. But Flora grew silent. She pushed her chair away from the table abruptly and went into the kitchen for more coffee.

"May I be excused?" I asked quickly.

"Yes," she said as she left the room.

"Good-night," my father said.

"Good-bye," said Randolf and reached out to shake hands.

"Bye-bye, honey bunch," said Adelaide. She put her arm around my waist as I stood by her chair and gave me a squeeze.

I flew to my room to get the message. I thought that it would divert Flora from her impatience with Adelaide.

I got the envelope from under my pillow and ran down the back stairs to catch her privately. I handed her the message.

"For me?" she said, and glanced at it with a laugh. "What a surprise. I had forgotten that was today."

"I am only the postal service," I said. "I am delivering it for someone else." I squirmed with delight. "Well, open it! Read it!"

She read through the message quickly. Then read a line or two again. She looked down at me.

"Who gave it to you?" in a low urgent voice.

"I can't tell. I promised."

She looked at the letter again. Then back at me. "Listen, are you sure this is for *me?* Are you *sure* the person meant it for *me?* Did the person say, 'Give it to Flora'? Did the person say my name?"

"No. The person said, 'Give it to *her* in a private moment.' "

It was delicious that she was bewildered. I had thought that she would be onto it in a flash.

She thought for a moment. Her expression altered slightly, became crafty. "Oh, of course. It's from your father. Yes? We are married people so it's from your father. Am I right?" She hoped to read my face.

I giggled. What fun!

"Listen here," she said desperately, grabbing my arm, "you've got to tell me more about this. You've *got* to!"

If I wasn't careful she would have the whole thing out of me in one more minute. I knew her.

"I'm not saying any more. I *promised*." I pulled away and fled.

> *Oh, you're the one I truly love,*
> *So won't you fly to me.*
> *Oh, you're the one and only love*
> *On ocean, land or sea.*
>
> *Just like the captain on his ship*
> *The Indian in his tent*
> *When I am all alone with you*
> *I count my time well spent.*
>
> *So won't you take this heart of mine,*
> *I wear it on my sleeve,*
> *A ruby red and beating heart,*
> *If only you'll believe.*
>
> *Be My Valentine.*

In the blank space below the verse, under the two hearts held up by Cupid, he had written in a firm but disguised hand, "Guess Who?"

HARLEY was crazy about barbecue sandwiches, and so, to satisfy his craving, a couple of times a week the three women, Dot, Flora and Tansy's mother, drove out along the highway till they came to Porky's Pig Parlor.

If I didn't have dancing classes or an invitation to play with a friend after school, Flora took me along.

Flora tried not to leave me alone with Sadie for any length of time. If I was watching Sadie iron or bake pies and my mother overheard the drone of Sadie's voice and the rise of my questions, it made her nervous. Sadie told me how people ought to behave and how things ought to be done. The resolutions of her stories delivered a moral precept, just as my father's did. Around her surged a raging maelstrom of hankerings, a turbulence of miscreants black and white, rich and poor. But Sadie was unmovable, a lone piling sunk deep into the bedrock of an unwavering moral certainty.

Sometimes though, if Sadie had something awkward to impart directly to me, something she did not want to be held responsible for having *told* me, she went about the telling in a special way. She made it a word puzzle–left spaces for verbs, dropped all the nouns, reversed syntax–and that's what she was doing lately.

There was no doubt about it. There was *something* Sadie thought I should know.

As Sadie's stories darkened in tone, as her delivery waxed more somber and my piping questions tapped at her unyielding trunk, Flora suddenly called from the sunroom or from upstairs for me to please find her the nail-polish remover or the cotton balls or to bring her some matches.

There *was* something I ought to know, needed to know. A question of magnitude to be asked. I just didn't know what it was yet. The formulation of the question gathered, the phrases rose to the surface of my mind, I could almost speak them, then they sank again, just out of reach.

This question had an answer all ready and waiting. I felt that if I could just speak the question, the answer would be immediately forthcoming. I could picture the answer as almost a physical thing: it would shine for me, a golden machinelike sculpture with many slender moving parts, different from every angle and yet the same. It would materialize to ride the air in front of me for all my days. It even had a name, this glimmering model, pasted to the base it floated on. It was called *Now You Know*.

WHEN we got to the Pig Parlor, Flora pulled into one of the spaces marked by slanted yellow lines painted on the concrete and tooted the horn.

Women didn't go into the Parlor, only men. Through the plate-glass window we could see the cooks and waiters in long white aprons stirring the stew of pork simmered so long it fel' away from the bones into the rich sweaty-smelling sauce, where it separated into threads of gravy-soaked flesh. The final color of the barbecue was a soft warm tan. The sandwich was composed of this thick brew spread onto a square, unheated bun, then wrapped in a thin paper with saw-tooth edges that soaked up the grease and spotted your clothes if it touched them.

When Flora sounded the horn one of the aproned men came out to poke his elbows through the car window, rest his chin on his crossed wrists and say, "How yawl?"

We had a barbecue while we waited for Harley's order, and when the man removed the metal tray from the side of the car we drove back into town to the car showroom, Dot holding the paper bag of hot meat.

Harley greeted the women.

"Here they are, hot and dripping, spicy and good to chew."

"For God's sake, Harley," said Dot with a smirk, "don't you ever have anything else on your mind?"

"Honey, I am gonna wear you out on this trip. You are gonna parlez with Harley, honey babe. Parlez with Harley all night long."

He glanced at me. "Hey, Shirley Temple, bring me three or four of those cups."

I pulled four of the paper cones from the dispenser by the water cooler.

Harley opened a desk drawer and removed a flask. Before he poured the shots into the cups he held two of them up to his chest, points outward, and fluttered his eyelashes. "Mother's milk to me. Mother's milk."

I went back to the cooler and pushed the button that caused the water to flow. I liked to see the heaving bubble inside the glass tank and hear the machine give its deep satisfying belch.

Flora was thrilled about the trip. She talked to Dot about what clothes she would pack, what hats to carry, shoes for dancing in the clubs at night and walking the strand at noon, and so on. Then she talked of the physical scene of the beach itself, how she had never been to the ocean, about the salt air, the shells, marshes, bracken. She began to bore them, I could tell, with her almost romantic musings.

"Flora, we're not going for the botany," said Dot.

"More toward biology, I'd say," from Harley.

"Come on, everybody! Let's leave right *now!*" shouted Dot suddenly. She dashed over to a roadster that was on display and scrambled behind the wheel, tightening her scarf against the wind. Tansy's mother chose a huge luxury sedan and turned to wave me a sad and soundless good-bye. The steering wheels were gripped, lips pursed. "Go!" exploded Dot, and they pretended to take off, heads jerking back against the force of the start as Dot made "brudden, brudden" sounds, her mouth vibrating with the emanations of air. They gave frantic arm and hand signals and leaned into the imaginary curves with exaggerated bends of the body. They "passed" each other time and again, tooting the car horns with wicked glee and all but splitting the plate-glass windows of the showroom with the din.

Harley and Flora still sat sipping whiskey in the office area, their voices covered by all the foolish commotion.

"Listen, sweetheart," said Harley. "Dot is good fun, there's some good grabbing there, I'm not denying that. But you and I, Flora, you and I are birds of a feather. We want just a leetle more than what the ordinary folks can get by with. We need to go a leetle beyond." He measured about a half-inch with his thumb and forefinger. "To fly a leetle higher, you get my meaning? Yeah? Am I right? I'm right, aren't I, doll?"

"I think, Harley," said Flora, "that a time comes when we are ready to give up on those longings. When life begins to make sense from another direction. It's just time to settle down and land somewhere and stop the high flying. Time to realize that things are okay the way they are, that there is a future right where we are."

"Then why are you heading in a certain direction, toward a certain area on the map where there is something that you 'used' to want? Are you kidding yourself, doll, that your car is going to stay on the right path? That your luscious body is going to fall for this stuff that your mind and your reason are trying to sell it? Your mind is pointing you in one direction but your wings are going to float you in another when you get near that turnoff. There's a reason you're going in your own car, and if you're honest you'll admit it. Now, here's what I'm telling you. If that doesn't work out, if you can't get from that source the satisfaction you need, well, let me offer my services. You can call on me and you won't regret it."

Flora listened to him transfixed. His very outrageousness seemed to beguile her. She tapped the sides of her shoes together soundlessly as she sat, head bent down, in one of the swivel chairs, her long legs stretched out in front of her.

"So what do you say? How 'bout we make an appointment for this trip? Have Delia get us a room and I'll think up a way to dodge around Dot for one night, okay? We'll try a little of the old flip and glide. I know a thing or two that'll spin your prop, honey. A couple of twists and rolls that'll take you to the clouds. All right? Are we on? Do a little work on those?" and he inclined his head toward the buttons on her jacket. Then he turned and blew a kiss toward Dot, encouraging the terrible racket they were making, assessed my interest in the water cooler, and returned his attention to Flora.

"My oldest sister had big knockers," he said. "Oh, yeah. I wanted to mess with them in the worst way. When I was about ten she fell in love with Jesus. She sang hymns like they were love songs." Harley's voice became a sugar scoop. "'And He *walks* with me and He *talks* with me, and He tells me I am His own, ta-da-da.' When she sang 'Abide with Me' she was really inviting Christ to set up house with her. Really put her heart into that one. Lord"—he laughed and shook his head—"she'd sing that stuff and sweat up a storm. Hot church, waving that palmetto fan, those boobs swinging and sliding. Top of her front"—he moved his palm up and down in front of his own chest—"was flat. Up at the top. Absolutely flat. Then down around the bottom of her rib cage, near her waist, here come those two big babies, nipples like chestnuts."

He leaned over and touched Flora's knee with the tip of his finger. "It's not so unusual for relatives to be interested in each other." He tilted back in his swivel chair again.

"Every Sunday afternoon I'd peek through the keyhole into her room and there she'd be, lying on the bed in her petticoat kissing the Nazarene. Had a color picture of Him, framed, sappy look on His face, long curls. You would have thought He was Rudy Vallee.

"My brother and me, we'd chase her. Try to tickle her, get her all gooseyed up and overheated, run her first one way and then the other, reach out for her and just graze those tits time and again. She would shriek and holler for Mama, half giggling, half hysterical. To tell you the truth I think she loved it." He paused. "Man, that was fun."

"What happened to her?" said Flora. Harley grinned as though she had taken the bait.

"Well, that's exactly what I want to tell you, doll. She found out about those nuns, you know, the Catholics? She heard that they are all considered the Brides of Jesus. They are married to Jesus." He stopped.

Flora looked at him, expressionless. "Well, what happened?"

"When she realized that we, the Baptists, didn't have that kind of a setup, she just sort of gave up on life. Figured she'd never be able to beat out the competition of all those Irishwomen and wops up in heaven, I guess." There were points of evil delight in his eyes. "You see, doll, they are in the *service* of *God* but spiritually *married* to *Jesus*. Sort of the condition you've worked out for yourself. But think of the waste. All those long, hot Sunday afternoons wasted. Makes me sad."

The other women tired of their game and after some car-door slamming returned to their drinks.

The group settled on leaving just after Easter, to get to the shore as spring crept up the coast and started to warm the sands and take over from the winter chill.

Flora kept to her scheme of driving alone in her own car, and Harley nodded approval. She strove to maintain some flexibility in her arrival date. She kept saying she would join them a day or so after they got there and that they shouldn't worry if they didn't hear from her as she drove on her way, that there might be a span of time when she would be out of touch.

"Hey, Flora," said Harley to my mother as she gathered her gloves and purse, "I hope to take you for a spin." He said this with a terrible, encouraged widening of the mouth.

I GOT a small package in the mail. Sometimes Randolf sent me a thick envelope filled with foreign stamps for my collection, but this time he sent a package with a gift and a note.

> Hello to you!
>
> I am sending you this bell for the handlebar of your scooter. Now that spring is almost here I expect you are out riding up and down the sidewalk in front of the house. Are you wearing out the soles of your shoes using your foot as a brake? I remember how Flora fusses at you for that. So here's a bell to warn passersby.
>
> And speaking of Flora, I'm wondering if that valentine found its way into her hands, somehow. *Could you let me know?* Our secret. Remember your promise!
>
> Your pal,
> Randolf

A gift required a thank-you note in return, and with his usual good manners Randolf had thought up two questions for me to answer to start off my letter and give me something to say. He always made my tasks easier for me. How I loved him!

To show my appreciation I would take my time with the thank-you note and exert myself to the limits of my calligraphy. I would write in my most perfect Palmer and illuminate the edges of the page with exquisite drawings. Every day in the late afternoon I labored over the page with crayons and pen.

As the days grew almost imperceptibly longer and the evenings milder, they still sat together, my mother and father, and talked of the future. Her future, really. The holdings, the contracts, the arrangements.

Some nights his natural ire with doctors got the best of him and he lost his train of thought—property—and steamed off into a damnation of medical practice.

"They do that kind of thing, doctors, keep you going for a few more days, then a few more, to increase their bill. They don't make enough money as it is, slicing up poor suckers who go in, innocently enough, for some minor operation and then are told they need another. And another. Don't give me over to their uses. Do you hear? Do you promise me? I don't want that."

She began to get home earlier in the afternoons and to wait with some impatience for my father's return from work. She greeted him, her eyes bright, and began to talk about business to him the minute he entered the house. She had things to say during dinner, all during the evening, and as they came up the stairs to bed. She chatted, she introduced topics, she didn't just respond as in the old days.

She began to practice adding columns of figures. She got a steno pad and timed herself taking notes to the announcer's voice on the radio. Then she re-created the entire speech and asked me, after she read it back, if she had reproduced it correctly. I listened to the announcer closely and to her rendition avidly. She was good.

She still talked on the phone about the trip, but the urgency had relented. Her commitment to it had evolved into something else. Her purpose, once insistent and pressing, had elided, was on hold.

Even so, one night she broached the subject of "the excursion," as she called it, to my father.

"I've never been to the ocean," she said. "Do you realize that I've never really been to the ocean? It's not as though I planned to go alone. I'll be with my friends," she said. "There'll be three women just like the time I went to the Charleston Gardens."

I heard no mention of Harley. Or of her driving alone.

My father didn't have a lot to say about the trip. Her fears had been that he would get into a rage and humph around in a ferocious temper, or worse, ask detailed questions about travel arrangements and companions. He didn't, though. He took the news quietly. There was a silence while he held his gray gaze on her face, learning God knows how much. "Go," he said softly. "If that's what you want."

RANDOLF'S letter was delivered with the news that he and Adelaide were engaged.

THE needle punctured her sides, her neckline, her spine. The machine treads pulled body parts under the point of steel and pierced hole after hole in them, threaded silk through them, outlined her form with them. Demented, she buttoned her nipples, tattooed her wrists, scissored between her legs.

She ripped half a torso from the machine and severed the vein and artery, two threads, with her teeth, a carnivorous snip, head to one side, light glinting from the moisture, the saliva that lay on a white incisor, the sparkle of a mouth ready to feed.

She refused to answer the phone, to receive visitors. Card games were skipped. Teas forgotten. Dot stranded. Harley unpampered.

She snatched a feather, a ribbon, held them to her waist, darted to the mirror, returned to fling them on the bed. She sat in her slip at the machine, pedaling furiously, suddenly dashing her head downward as though to bite through the Singer itself, instead closed one of her eyes, aimed, and jabbed the point of a new color strand into the open eye of the needle. After a whirlwind of movement she observed her full-length reflection, fully clothed now, poised, a hand on one hip, holding a glove, wearing the other. A graceful turn, an adjustment of the veil, and then with a keen cry of impatience, she ripped one whole side of the garment from her body and crammed it into the machine again.

She was both building a creature and devouring it, absorbing it. Creator and cannibal. She molded a persona, a shade, a seductress. She was seeking her own true form, her own true configuration, silhouette, colors—if only she could find the drape of the shoulder, the hang of the skirt, the hue of the frock, the right stockings, shoes, pin, scarf, if only she could incorporate the coat, the fur, the jewel to compose the true and only perfect way to look, then she would know, she would surely find, she would call out at last, her own, her only, her one true mate.

JUST before Easter there was a snow that came when the buds and blossoms were already on the trees. A night of frozen stars gave way to a dawn of white crystals. The whole galaxy had splintered, cracked and fallen from the sky. The dawn appeared, gray, but with traces of pink afterbirth trailing the once-laden clouds. A dawn of glaze, of frosted water, a dawn that stopped the spring, sealing into briefly preserved youth, rot and decay. Sealing into suspended promise, the hurried ruin of melt and thaw.

SADIE refused to wait until the car pulled away from the curb. By this time she was on the verge of mutiny. She was barely civil. She brought the hatboxes as asked, stood fidgeting while Alexander made room for them in the rear, and the minute he took the last one from her grasp, made a point of wiping her hands on her apron so that my mother saw.

It was late morning, the sun had returned and the air was soft.

I had been out of school for several days with grippe, had lain in bed with a fever while my mother put the finishing touches on her wardrobe. She had given me scraps of the various fabrics and trims she used, and I wrapped them with desultory fingers around the bodies of my dolls. Then, losing interest or lacking the skill to fulfill my vision of couture on such thickset manikins, I dropped the swaddled figures on the bedspread, where they lay puffing it into a quilt of colors. I stared out the windows at the birch trees and their catkins, the ornamental crab apples, each bloom bearing a birthmark of rust from the freeze.

When my fever began I had coughed, sniffled, and glowed into a source of heat. My mother was finally forced to place her palm on my forehead and accept the fact that I was indeed sick. She gave my face a quick study. How long will this take? Not long, she must have decided, and moved foward with her plans. Sure enough, the high fever ran itself out and in two days I was normal, but weak.

She had popped into my room as I lay baking, appearing in sundry states of dress and undress, to check my progress, and I in return checked hers. The afternoon frocks were coming along. The evening dresses were satisfactory, although the shoes were iffy. The lingerie no problem, it had been chosen in the shops. She was taking a mountain of clothes—garments suited not only to the weather in its present state, early spring, but summer things, sandals, halter tops.

It was startling at one point to see through the haze of my fever that she had suddenly gone bald. She wore swimsuit, beach robe, and in her relentless attention to detail had tucked her hair up under a white rubber bathing cap embossed with marceled curls and waves. She measured me with her glance, then went to the mirror to check shoulders and buttocks and to insert a pointed finger up under her pants, loosening the thigh-grip of the spandex.

As I mended she packed. For each degree drop another layer was added to her cases. Such restraint was an altogether unprecedented display of manners on her part. I knew she would go regardless.

My mistake was in assuming she intended to come back.

I HAD on my winter coat, a stranger to me after my several days in bed. I explored the pockets. What I hoped for was a diversion, an exciting, distracting discovery that would take me into the first five minutes of her long absence. I found only that small species of semiorganic creature, the pocket crumb. Some of them crept under my fingernails and I brought them out into the light to peer at them in captivity.

"All right," she said. "I think that's everything."

"Yes, ma'am," said Alexander. He nodded several times, waiting to see if she had last-minute thoughts. "Yes, ma'am." Then he went over to a row of bushes and scraped under them with his rake. The iris were coming up.

She smoothed the back of her skirt with the tops of her hands as she bent to sit behind the wheel. She adjusted the cuffs of her traveling suit, settling her shoulders several times to make certain her arms were free. She had on kidskin gloves and a navy felt hat secured with a puckered ribbon that sneaked under the bun of her dark hair. She turned her head from side to side as she looked into the rearview mirror, checking visibility around the hatboxes. As she placed her purse on the passenger seat I heard the jingle of her bracelets. The case with her cosmetics and perfumes, a beguiling miniature of the larger luggage, sat smugly on the rear seat where I usually rode.

She took a mental inventory of the boxes, luggage, their contents, that satisfied her. She turned the ignition key on its metal loop with sporty leather tab. The motor chugged in response and the car began to quiver with anticipation.

"All right," she said, looking straight ahead. "I'm leaving."

And then I knew. I knew she really was. She was leaving.

I watched the car move away, the plume of its exhaust, the shine of light on its body. When it was out of sight I considered the gray-brown pebbles of the highway. They were embedded in, held fast by concrete to make a path for my mother's car to travel along. I followed, until it turned the corner, the white line down the center of the street that guided the car, that was to keep it in its lane all the way to South Carolina. The line was to lead the car down from the foothills of crisp air, spring flowers, sparkling streams to the plains where cotton and tobacco would soon be planted, then into piney woods, over the black sluggish waters of bayous, onto silver roads winding between beckoning gray moss, to marshes, to delta, magnolias, palmettos, to the hot strip of beach, to warmth, to humidity, to heat, to salt, to the place where there is no snow, to the tropics, to the warm place, to the place where there is no ice, to the place where ice cannot be sustained, to the place where all ice melts.

The street split open at my feet. The giant boulders that lay beneath the earth, the firm mammoth rocks which bore on their steady backs the comings and goings of our daily lives, the foundation on which the house, the yard, the town itself rested, screeched with pain and tore apart like paper. A scalding wind rose from the chasm. My feet left the ground as a crashing blow broke my spine, snapped my shoulders, cracked my skull. I was lifted, hurled into black space. Hot venom bubbled into my mouth. I tumbled, blind. I fell, torched. I hurtled, whipped and stung, swords of flame, needles of ice, deaf, blind, mutely screaming.

I turned, my hands in my pockets, and went up the walk toward the wide front door. I opened it and pushed it so that it swung on its hinges silently inward. I went into the stone house.

SIX

THE return addresses were route numbers. "Rural Route 2, Valdese," or "Rt #4, Maiden, N.C." If letters came they had wrinkles, smudges, purple three-cent stamp in the corner, waves of lines canceling it. More often a penny postcard, cheaper. "We are fine tho' Hub's mama broke her arm Tues dr says it will heal up alrite, carried Bernice over to Grace Baptist last evening hoping to see Clyde and Aunt Garnette they wasn't there tho'."

Flag the Trailways bus, the C&NW, mostly freight, town people snickered when you rode it. Shoe-box lunch, fried chicken, deviled egg, fat, gray-green pickle, warts on it, made you feel funny to circle it with your mouth, didn't know why, though. Save the shoe box, there aren't many that come into the house.

Stand and look out the door, look out the door, soft rain falling, porch tilts down on one corner, mule-eared chair, seat-bottom dropping. Floorboards have frayed edges, she's barefoot, she can't stand her dress her hair her home her hopes. A chicken cackles, Burt snuffles in the barn—his day off—sees slattern Jessie out across the field dart into the woods, someone's old pickup takes off, gears in geriatric complaint. Sunday, Sunday.

FLORA drove well. She held the wheel with her right hand. On the straightaways she draped her left elbow out the open window;

her fingers occasionally rose to touch her hair. If she smoked she held the cigarette so that the glow of flame was reflected in the windshield and the smoke streamed to obscure her view. She arranged this hazy aspect to soften the edge of the hard red countryside. The red-clay banks of the shoulders and cutdowns at the side of the road offended her somehow. They seemed organic and nasty, an inner view of the earth that was too intimate, that shouldn't be revealed to just any passing stranger. A scalpeled view that only a farmer ought to have, a person involved in the care of the earth; the washouts that gave sight of contorted roots, nourished on only one side, the glimpse of fence post or mailbox stake forced deep into the belly of the land.

She thought about her days of nurse's training before the man had lured her away, courted her, and married her. Of the time he spotted her and another student nurse on the street of the town, leapt from the car, removed his hat and introduced himself, saying to her, "You'll see me again," then returned to his car, not insulting them by offering them a ride—that would have been too forward—and sped away. The startled girls laughed, their arms around each other's waists, clasping each other in hysterical giggles, thinking him a funny old man. She had been impressed, though, by the compressed energy of him.

As she drove she read the billboards. She noticed the barns, the chicken coops. The corner of a feed-sack curtain blowing through a screenless window told her all she needed to know about life in that farmhouse: the thin walls with mice between them, the flowers on the wallpaper, the sounds that came through the walls; the cold dinners of beans and corn bread. She knew about the pails of heated water poured into a tin tub and the scrubbing of each other's back, familiar as one's own could never be. The intimacy with someone else's garments, with siblings' bodies, with a parent's every possession. That mixture of loathing and comfort produced by the familiar, the overknown. Each particular teaspoon. The contents of every box, the pictures of every worn magazine. Newborn farm animals were a miracle of freshness, had the possibility, perhaps, of astonishing, but after a while even they performed according to genetic command and refused to become other than a replication of their parents, their kind.

Only her father, Rawlings, had the power to amaze, the ability to fascinate her endlessly with his life, his joy, his comings and goings, bursting through the door, stamping his boots. His laughter, his music. He took her out of that dreary world into a place of electricity and alertness.

They went to a hillbilly music show once, in the schoolhouse, all ten children, the two parents, hair slicked, walking down the edge of the road, saw people, crowd gathering, saw people, paid for tickets, took up a whole row. Men played fiddles, banjos, smacked big thumping bass like flesh slapped. She felt stirrings, musical phrases made their way toward resolution, men tapped toes in time, sang mournful songs in high wailing voices, told jokes, put on and took off hats, waved bandana handkerchiefs, grins showed corn-kernel teeth, low-class, silly. One performer had huge safety pins up the front leg of his overalls, another asked him, "Why?" Answer: "That's my cane holder," and to demonstrate he put his walking cane through the series of pins, the handle curved between his legs just where the male member must have been located under those same pants. How embarrassing, she told herself, he's not aware of that. Minnie stood up, bolt upright, outraged, led them all out of the row of seats, up the aisle, out of the auditorium. The audience snickered at them, their all standing up in the middle, and even though they had paid their money Minnie led them out of the place and down the highway. They walked home, the little ones crying, "Why, why?" till slapped. They never went to another show again. At all. Ever.

She felt herself hollow-boned, airborne. Only an occasional tightening in her shoulders caused her to stop the car and walk off into the growing things by the road, examine reeds, cattails, the sort of vegetation that surrounded the marshes and bogs. She snapped open seed pods and let the embryonic globes roll around in the palm of her hand, tiny planets. Their circulations stirred her, took her heat and grew dryer, leaving on her flesh wet specks, the fluid of germination.

THE whorl of his ear, the length of his neck, the place where the ribs fuse into an arch and draw the skin taut. To run the tip of the tongue, to outline with the tongue the crest of fused ribs. Lick along the spine and down, tongue darting and dipping, hot breath, a hot crevice, deeper, deeper in the rich brown fermenting taste, then the hot, contained, mercury weight of his balls, then the root into her mouth, into her sucking mouth.

He would try the place that was too tight, grasping her hips, pulling her, bent over, backing her toward him, the saddle of her hips. Slight rips, tears, fissures. Stinging lesions as he pushed and spurted.

Surely a longing of such intensity and duration confers on the one who yearns some claim, some rights of ownership.

At noon the next day she passed a tavern by the side of the road. It was the first scheduled meeting place for the group.

Harley was ushering the other two women in through the door when he spotted the dark red coupe on the highway. He lifted an arm in greeting and broke into a smile. Off to the rear of the tavern were cabins for rent. She didn't even slow down, just passed by, her head not turning. She saw in the mirror the O of Harley's mouth as he continued to say her name.

She came to a detour sign and saw a convict work gang, guards with rifles, hounds on the leash, men wearing wide stripes and ankle irons. A two-wheeled black coffin of bubbling tar stood to the shoulder of the road, its vapors medicating the air. Some distance out in a field, parked under a tree, top-heavy in its construction, there was what first appeared to be a jaunty circus wagon or the traveling home of a gypsy family. Bars on the sides, rolled canvas, iron wheels, padlock on the door gave rise to thoughts of pacing animals or the telling of fortunes. Then she saw a corner of mattress ticking, the wilt of a filthy blanket, and realized that she had sighted the sleeping cage where the men were chained at night.

Flora opened her window and took the signal flag that was thrust toward her. She was to carry it, she knew, around the curve of the road and relinquish it to the man posted there. But her impulse was to keep it, to run with it, to hold it as passport or proof that she had been given leave to travel, freedom to fly away.

WHEN she called, Randolf agreed to meet her on the deserted beach, taking the afternoon from his work and driving miles to get there. Flora was unable to read his expression, but that had long ago ceased to confound her. Now she worked to control hers. She knew that he would hear what she had to say, listen with his head bent as though searching for a lost object among the sea wrack, and that when he raised his head it would be to gaze out over the ocean at the gulls.

He had kissed her, precisely, on the cheek when they greeted. It was not the kiss of a young man who has declared himself a lover. It was the kiss, however, given by a young man, fastidious in grooming and whose shoes and cuffs now sank into a foaming tide; a young man, conscientious and exacting, who had rushed from his desk leaving a hasty and flimsy excuse; a young man, betrothed, but whose fiancée had no knowledge of his whereabouts.

She reckoned this evidence and she began to talk. The sun at their backs gave them the illusion of warmth as they walked and cast their shadows, elongated and pulsating, before them.

"In the summer, in the country, we chopped cotton," she

said. "Or hoed potatoes or baked bread in a stove so hot it singed our hair. Or stirred boiling wash in a pot, or ironed or churned till our arms ached, or peeled fruit for canning and fought off the yellow jackets that waded in the juice on our wrists. In summer gnats follow you, midges try to land in your eyes, squat like toads on the iris, think they've found a swimming hole. Sweat bees plague you, the dust that squirms up between your toes is a living thing, filled with ticks, chiggers, hookworm, ringworm. Your hair sticks to your neck, wet salt crawls down your back. Your spent breath leaves an organic trail where you've walked—like one of the horses, or a dog. If a stranger happens to come around he doesn't have to ask where your privy is located. He knows. The milk cows out in the pasture are covered with flies, and when they drop their dung the wasps are in it, the beetles, almost before it hits the ground. It turns crisp, dries, turns to ash, while you watch. By afternoon all I could think of was the river. Before Minnie finally let me quit I had one last order. To get the fresh-churned butter to the springhouse before it turned rancid. I'd put the crock in the shed and then I'd dip for myself a cold drink of water. I'd prolong for a minute the joy of pulling my dress over my head and cooling my body with a swim. Sometimes in there, in the shed in a dark corner, I'd hear a rustle or see a jerking, twisted sort of movement . . . some small, sick creature had crept in, found a cool place to die.

"The river was narrow, with high slick red banks. There was a group of rocks just upstream of where I swam, and the rushing of the water over those cut down on the leeches, water fleas. But I'd see turtles, fish, crawdads. The water was brown, murky, busy carrying away Rawlings' topsoil. I had to feel for the bottom, learn the oozy spots, the sharp stones, slick moss patches. I had one or two favorite areas where there was sand, but that was unreliable. After heavy rains it was gone, washed downstream.

"Minnie told me to wear my petticoat when I swam, for modesty—if my sisters ever came with me, they did. They liked the white of them in the water, thought they looked like water lilies or something. Proud of their bits of ruffle or some pitiful scrap of ribbon that had survived Minnie's scrubbing. I wouldn't wear anything, though, because the white of the petticoats billowing reminded me of Queen Anne's lace. A weed. Grows anywhere; the more sorry the soil, the hotter the summer, the more it blooms. I would not be Queen Anne's lace. Not out of modesty, not from Minnie's command, not for anybody. I swam naked.

"One day when I was alone, or thought I was, I looked toward the rapids and I saw him. Coming downstream like a bullet, his brown body waving, curling through the water, around the rocks. I saw the forked tongue. I saw the pits on the side of his head. He left the rapids and hung for a second, just hung, in the air, almost over my head, three feet, maybe four feet long. A cottonmouth. On his way to the frog pond down in the hollow. He dove in beside me. Hardly made a splash. A moccasin wants to own the river when he uses it. Likes to search around, shorten his trip, find dinner where he is. They resent noise and confusion, get frightened, strike.

"I should have stayed still, or slowly moved toward shore, grab a root or tree branch and haul myself out, but I didn't. That day I wanted the river as much as the snake did. And if the only way I could have it was to share it, then that's what I would do. I stayed in. I stayed in and I stretched out on that muddy water and I swam. That's what I've come to tell you. When I want something, that's what I can do. That's how far I can go. I can swim with the snake, Randolf. Can you?"

M Y father and Sadie divided me. Lily Mae got the leftovers.
Sadie placed before me for my diversion a wad of
dough. I was to bake a tiny pie for my dessert while she made a
real one for my father.

My hair felt lank, it still hadn't been shampooed since my
grippe. I thought of Rose's beauty shop and Mattie's skull-
popping fingers. The dough got grayer and grayer as I alternately
patted it and scratched my head.

"Dogs run them down, that's how," said Sadie. "They can't
excape. Run them to earth. Hounds don't get tarred like them
boys do. Hounds keep they legs goin' sunup to sundown and far,
way far, beyond. Sheriff's dogs run them boys down."

"But why do they do bad things? Why do people do bad
things if they know they'll have to go to prison or the work farm
or be locked on the chain gang? Why do they take razors to each
other if they know the sheriff'll catch them and the guard'll shoot
them if they try to run away? Why do they drink whiskey and
fight and gamble?"

" 'Cause they's mens. That's what the mens does. They's
mean and full of sass. They riles up in a hurry."

The blades are silver and sharp and fast. One slash on the
arm and red blood spurts. The victim is full of surprise. "Why,

look at that! It wasn't there a second ago. Where did that come from?" Wonder on his face, he lifts his head to share his news. Lifts his head and bares the vulnerable stalk of his neck, his throat. A burning line crosses it and he falls. Or, if he lives, he bears forever the swollen, clumsy mend of keloid healing, a bulging purple shine, the permanent formality of a necktie woven of his own flesh.

The juice trickled along her wrists as she spoke. She dropped the stems and pits into the colander, cherries into a bowl.

"How do they not get lost? How do they know the way home if they've never been in that place before?"

"They knows how to follow the sun or the stars. They looks at the Dipper, they sees where the sun come up. They 'member where they home is, where the sun come up when they home, and they lights out that way."

"What if it's cloudy? A cloudy day?"

"They spit on they thumb and then polish it up good and hole it up to the light and that ole sun shine on the fingernail and give them they direction that way. You kin catch the light of the sun most any day no matter how it clouded over."

She put more flour into the dough. When she kneaded the crust pastry the flour worked its way up her arms and she got whiter and whiter. She had white-person hands and arms and black-person everything else.

"What do they eat? How do they keep from starving?"

"They catches them a turnip out behind the prison kitchen. Half rotten. Been throwed out. They puts they dinner bread under they shirt. Once they on the run they picks up acorns or scuppernongs, but mostly what they wants is water. They runnin' too hard to eat. Make they stomach cramp. That boy gets home his mama fry him up a chicken real good."

"How do the sheriff and his men find them in all those woods? How can they catch them if they have a head start?"

"Well, that prison place sets still. It don't go nowhere, so that sheriff and his men, they know they surroundings. They put a man call a 'stander' at the gap, place where you gots to cross through, narrow place where you can't go no further, gots to go forward or back. Stander have him a gun. Have him a big rifle. Back at the prison yard they give that strike dog the scent. They hole them dogs on leashes and follow them dogs, and the meanest of all is a strike dog that don't howl. That don't squall like a baby when it find live trail. It keep it mouth shut and the poor boy who runnin' don't know how close they is. He stop for water or to find his way, or to catch his breath, and them dogs *on* him. All over him.

"Peoples what do wrong, they be punish. He to the penitentiary if he still be alive."

She paused a moment to watch the ripples of that remark widen. "You go on now," she said. "Lily Mae goin' be here soon play cards with you."

I got the cards out of the drawer where my mother kept them and chose my favorites. They were of an extraordinary shiny stiffness and illustrated with a lavish gathering of flowers, full-blown, so mature that some petals had been released from the blossoms and drifted in front of a lush velvet drapery that hung behind the vase. I wondered where that place could be, where flowers and drapery achieved such remarkable fruition and exuberance. Where was it that artists lived? It must be a land different from the town I knew. It must be a country of contentment, where each citizen felt cherished and the people dressed in satins and silks encrusted with lace. Stately beings who walked with the carriage of statues.

CONTENTMENT. It was a condition I longed to observe. I wondered what it looked like. I watched people closely, I thought, but I had never seen one who appeared content. Of course, Adam and Eve had been content in the Garden of Eden for a while. And God had been content when He created the Garden and the world. Then the first people sinned and were driven away from the place where, briefly, they had been content. But instead of destroying the people who had angered Him and starting all over with two new contented people who might do better, God let the banished pair have babies. Who all grew up to be discontent. And they in turn had more discontented babies. And God became known as a God of wrath and vengeance because discontented people kept making Him mad.

It could have been so easy, I thought, for God to have made Adam and Eve disappear and to create another couple. And to have put *them* into the Garden to try out human beings again. Why was He withholding contentment not only from man but from Himself? I wondered.

Contentment must be put together out of a very complicated formula, I decided. Some slippery kind of process that keeps trickling out of the mind. Even God's mind. And when He roared into anger and lifted His godly finger to point Adam and Eve to the gate of Eden, to drive them out, at the same time, by mistake, He also drove out of His memory the formula for creating contentment. And of course there were no contented people to observe anymore. So God has kept creating new babies hoping one of them will grow up content and He can watch it and say, "Oh, yes. That's how I did it. *Now* I remember." But so far that hasn't happened.

If God has forgotten how to create contentment, I realized, then there cannot be a heaven. God has given man a false promise. What a terrible secret for Him to have to keep. There can only be a circling of risen souls in the high air, the restless beating of wings, a never-ending flight of tired, nervous, deceived souls, waiting for release and etching their pain on the blackness of night as they fly about the head of a frustrated, tormented, lying God.

I found some comfort, though, in the thought that roaring

through God's body, too, reverberating with every breath He takes, with every pulse that throbs, is the renewed knowledge of the causation, ownership and burden, the need for suppression, of a terrible guilt.

I ATTEMPTED to lay the cards out just the way Flora did, with that little snap of a fingernail at the corner on the moment of release, but they slithered and landed askew in ragged rows on the tabletop. I knelt to place them on the rug instead, observing the faces of the king, queen, and jack, whom I thought of as my father, mother, and Randolf. There were no pictures of me. I had tried to think of myself as the ace, which could be the highest or lowest, but it didn't seem right. I felt more comfortable as the two.

The day wore on. Lily Mae's visit brought scant pleasure. We played concentration and Lily Mae won.

When she left I picked up the cards, gathering them idly at first and then carefully when I remembered that they were among my mother's "best." I brushed the rug fuzz off them and counted them slowly, putting them in stacks of tens. There should be five piles of tens and two cards left over. There was only one card left over. I searched with mounting trepidation under chairs and cushions, finally finding it, an ace. Its plump red heart lay pounding softly under the fringe of the carpet. I pulled it out and held it.

WE glued white cotton onto George's head, surreptitiously licking the crusted paste from our fingers. We read of the firewood, each log a Joan of Arc, cheerful in self-immolation, providing light so that Abe could turn in his homework. In an orgy of raids on the supply room we took reams of construction paper in red and white for valentines.

"Now," the teacher had said, "I don't want to hear one

word about sweethearts. That has nothing to do with the way we celebrate this minor holiday. In this classroom we send valentine greetings to each other to get practice in spelling, vocabulary, and, just as important, to make amends for perhaps having hurt someone's feelings or having neglected them so far during the school year." She cleared her throat and spat into her handkerchief with little red hearts embroidered on it.

"I do not want to hear snickers or see fingers pointed or to overhear the name of any boy being linked with that of any girl. Furthermore, I do not want to find out that there is a person in this class who has left out sending a greeting to any of his or her classmates. Now line up and place your valentines in the box. No talking."

The teacher's attitude, her spinster's insistence that a valentine be considered more an expression of regret for past neglect than an outright declaration of romantic love was, I had told myself, what caused me to carry Randolf's valentine without hesitation to Flora.

But it wasn't.

I had thought about it. Actually, it was not so much that I had thought about it as that I knew there was something I didn't want to think about. So, most of the time when I almost thought about it, I was able to dismiss it. Or I only thought about it in glancing-off, grazing-the-edges kinds of ways.

I thought about it in terms of arithmetic and trying to form the more equal and therefore more equanimous pair. If I subtracted my mother's age from my father's there was a big number left over. If I subtracted Randolf's age from Flora's, however, only a little number remained. That made Randolf and Flora more equal. That gave indication of who belonged with whom, in a way, I thought.

Or I considered it as a punishment for my father when he frightened me with his temper. I mulled it over as a distraction, as a defense, as retaliation, even, on those Sunday rides when my father grew cross, then angry, then rapidly enraged with Flora. I hated the contortions of his round face, the way his eyes squeezed tight and hard, the ropes and pulleys of his neck.

Time and again, after the prayers, the polite handshakes with the pastor, the smiles and greetings given in Sunday sunshine, we got into the car and, in that enclosure with its own weathersphere, clouds gathered, instant gloom, the first drops began to fall, splashing heavy and hard onto the still-ruddy bloom of his salutations, the scattered daisies of her social chat. And before we had driven a block, the downpour.

It was his suits, she said. He didn't like to buy new ones—didn't want, I suppose, to be surprised out of his settled-upon self-image. He wore his old ones, still full in their fiber, still heavy in their weight of wool, solid goods but with each passing year sliding further out of style, dating him, labeling him eccentric; or so she would have him believe.

She told him they made a silly-looking couple—his relics of garments so opposite to her strutting good fashion (as she walked next to him, she intimated, taller, younger, full of juice). Their appearance beside each other, she said, *that* was the cause of the merriment, those grins of wicked glee. So she worried at him about his clothes, took a critical nip at a wrinkled flank, a too-wide cuff, a length of sleeve, till he raged into impatience, a bull baited, and turned to gore her, silencing her with a slashing command.

Sometimes I even thought I could see her point. If they were so unequal in years, one way to tidy up the difference *was* to appear as much alike as possible. My problem was that I liked the way each of them dressed. I loved her chic frocks, her open-toed shoes. But then I was reassured by the soft gray-and-white pinstripe of his suits, his vests, his fedora.

But she wasn't shouting, frightening me. He was. I wanted to fetch a mirror and hold it in front of his face, irrefutable proof of his ugliness in anger. I wanted some sort of machine to record his voice so that later, in a moment of calm, I could force him to listen to it. I longed to take him aside and, as we stood in a private, ivy-covered alcove somewhere, patiently explain just how awful shouting caused him to appear. Then, wisened, shocked, remorseful, contrite, seeing the truth of what I said (I saw myself in professional garb, mortarboard hat, it was a university setting), he gave his pledge of honor to cultivate a more gentlemanly and chivalrous style. I then, with relief, returned–child again–to the backseat of the car and to blameless and unwavering parental loyalty. Because when they argued, when he shouted, that's when I thought about it. About rewarding Flora. About Randolf and Flora as a pair. About the three of us, Randolf, Flora, and me, living in peace, in the changeless, smooth calm of Randolf's unwavering clime.

Most of the time, though, it was something I didn't want, and then it was easier not to think about it. It was easier to hide from it. Intuition warned that if I ever thought about it too much, thought about it as real, it would become real instead of only something to think about. And now it *had* become real; I must have thought about it once too often. Everywhere I looked, no matter where I turned, I saw it. Before my eyes. In my thoughts. Always preceding me, causing my intestines to slither and glide around each other, oiled by the sticky glistenings of guilt. I saw an embodiment, a materialization, a sort of sculpture. A metallic thing with many interlocking, intricate but somehow brutal moving parts that would ride the air in front of me for all my days. This sculpture was the answer to my question. It was called *Now You Know*.

"COME on," said my father and we went to the car. We headed out along the highway that we usually took to my grandparents' house, and then he slowed to read a road sign. This was flat country and not an area he enjoyed scenically, so he was unfamiliar with the roads. He took a turnoff that led to a small forlorn town, a county seat off to the east.

I read the road sign with him or tried to. Typical of adult logic, the sign gave the traveler data of his destination only when he was already approaching it. If a person were in a distant place and wanted to return to our town, the person would not find the name of it listed anywhere. You had to almost *be* there before you were told how to *get* there.

In the hard afternoon light we circled the courthouse square and saw the two groups of men who had tacitly divided the green. The white group, seated on slat benches, wore their Sunday suits of stiff, ungiving stuff. Some distance away the blacks stood, leaning, using for support the outside of a building where inside, at one time or another, most of them had been brought to their knees. They wore the clean overalls which they would dirty day by day in the fields all the coming week. The cannon at forty-five degrees pointed north, its stacked pyramid of ball ammunition long since petrified awaiting the order to counterattack.

We parked under a canopy of maples, droplets of their sap making splats of stickiness on the body of the car, and entered a brick residence.

It was the smell of the place that I noticed first—urine and the sick sweet of adult feces. Someone had had an accident in the front hall. We stepped past, my father regal in his overlooking of the mess. Old voices quavered hymns from the parlor. We were led to an upstairs room and paused in the doorway.

His head had gotten smaller. He had been placed in a cane-seated wheelchair, but since he no longer bent in the middle he seemed only to touch it with the back of his head and the bulge of his spine. One eye worked. He held a spoon in a funny way, and his tray of food perched on the outer reaches of a thin thigh. As we walked in the door the tray slipped and my father caught it.

He was crying.

"Oh, he's sad today," said an attendant in a white dress. "He broke his teacup. He really did like that teacup. I'm trying to cheer him up, show him the nice animals in the *National Jew-agraphic* but he don't pay no attention." She vacated her chair for my father. "We tried to fix it up for him, but you know, you can't mend a teacup hardly at-all. I put some Duco smint on it and set it up on the chiffonier where he can look at it but he don't understand he can't drink out of it no more. He just cries and cries."

The roommate was a quiet heap in a hospital bed, face turned to the wall. My gaze slid from the men as the tray again slid from the lap. The floor and baseboards were oak, the wallpaper feeble flowers. There were two closets. It must have been an elegant home once. Maybe it had belonged to the judge from the courthouse. I went to the window to see what his children had viewed on hollow Sunday afternoons. More maple trees, a garden with a now decrepit summer house, dainty wrought-iron chairs with a design of twisted vines. A screened porch for Parcheesi and jacks on rainy days.

Added to one corner of the room and making the space more hospital and less old bedroom was a lavatory. I went to examine it. Stopper on a chain. Separate hot and cold taps, which meant that the water couldn't be blended. The vulnerable soaped-up hands were either frozen or scorched. In this situation I always rushed my hands back and forth between taps in a disordering experience of opposites, too hot then too cold, too hot then too cold. The alternative was to draw water from both and then dip into a pool that lapped in the tainted basin where saliva and toothpaste had just been expelled.

The old men washed up while it was still partly dark. I imagined their sagging bodies in the dank, early morning chill, partly disrobed; those permanently semibent elbows of the elderly held away from the body for balance; the wisps of their slicked hair, shaved wattles. The fleeting roses that scrubbing lent their cheeks shone above the unthinkable secrets of their lathered, aging manhood.

In the past I had seen him come in from a morning's plowing and clean up in the fresh outdoors, as he must have done from childhood till illness. In the manner of a primitive or of a creature.

I found it easy to see kinship to animal in a country man—a man who has grown up washing his sweaty face, neck and hands out of doors in a basin of water drawn from a well or urged from a pump and then left in the sunlight to warm. He will splash and dip and slather himself, naked to the waist, the woman a shadow figure, glancing to the yard to check his progress. He will not be admitted to her kitchen to eat until he has met her standards. So, like a dog or a bird, he scoops water to his head and tosses it, or to his fledging wings and tries them, or like the summer swimming-hole boy he dives, drowns and gasps, all from the contents of a shallow dish placed on a rough board shelf over the bare earth of a workyard baking in the summer sun.

He made a sound and held out his hand to the chiffonier.

My father got the teacup down and handed it to him. It had a picture of two children on it, a boy and a girl in a sunny meadow. Glue bubbles clung to the brown hair that marked the cup into halves, the handle in thirds.

My father unwrapped a Hershey bar and broke it into bits. He put the bits into the teacup, and Rawlings put the cup to his lips. He shook it and candy dropped into his mouth. He smiled.

"Happy birthday, Rawlings," said my father. "Happy birthday."

We were in the room for a while, it could hardly be called a visit. But we waited out the time period that convention deemed adequate. When we were ready to go, I kissed him on the forehead and for a minute he was alive again.

Toleration time does not vary. The same people who had arrived as we did were gathered in the front hall ready to depart with empty food containers, bundled laundry, and relieved expressions. There was a shiny spot on the floor where the mess had been.

"Here's the bird," the lady in the white dress said to my father. "We told him he could have the home's canary in his room for his birthday, but I don't know if he'll even notice."

"Do it anyway," said my father.

When we got home at dusk, my father scrutinized the telephone carefully, as if by concentrating his thoughts on it he could tell whether it had rung while we were out. Because, of course, today was his birthday, too.

MYSTERIOUS strangers. Every small town has its arrivals who creep into residence, bringing with them secrets of great significance. Life-destroying secrets that bend the spine, sully the reputation. Secrets that are bile to their owners but of salient sweetness to their fellow citizens. How dearly loved is that fruit, that special fruit borne only on the Tree of Mistakes. How the gossiping mouth longs for it, to roll it on the tongue, savor its juice, crush the pulp, then spit the pits, willy-nilly, up and down Main Street.

The household where the family tree has sprouted into this other tree–twisted trunk, strange foliage, exotic leaf, unwanted fruit–will have chosen to transplant. They find a new town usually much like the old, set up in a neighborhood of no singularity, and, trembling, tentative, take up a life around the edges of life. These families seldom tell you where they lived before. On holidays they have few if any visitors. Their attempts to be "just like everybody else" are so strained that they are immediately remarked as different.

There was, in our town, such a family: war-torn refugees from the flying shrapnel of cutting talk, the soft, thudding bombardments of elbow nudges.

Residence can be changed, but human nature cannot. Local gossips had the scenario written before the moving van drove off.

The family must have sat one evening, it was told, around the kitchen table in their own town–father, mother, unmarried daughter–and agreed to transmute the unacceptable about the daughter into (what was universally thought to be) the impossible for the mother.

The daughter's mistake, a child a year behind me in school, was told that the older couple were her parents, the grown daughter her sister.

The compassionate father, his old job renounced, his pension forfeited, lived and worked in a gray disorientation and decline of spirit. The wife, hair white, bosom descending behind bib apron, moved with tired, muddled steps to retrace a path already traversed. Her martyr's eyes spun from incredulous neighborhood stares when the child addressed her as "mother."

The unmarried daughter, a quiet, nervous young woman, a seamstress, came straight home after work, had no friends, kept to her room–smoking, reading, staring at the wall, adding up her unrepayable debt.

The little girl could be seen trailing the older "sister" with her eyes. Or playing on the scraggly lawn among the roots and rocks, laying tea for her dolls on bare patches of ground, using a broken set, or, often, kneeling, to poke at nothing with a stick.

She started out fresh in school as we all did, eager, but adults foretold for her a falling away, an eventual turning. So far, though, she continued alert. Shy, withdrawn, petite, she managed. She took silent joy.

The day after my father's birthday, the day after my mother didn't call, I sought her out. When I found her, I pulled her aside, and as she shook her head, tears splashing first on one shoulder then the other, I said aloud to her, about her family, all the things she didn't ever want to have to know.

SEVEN

 LATE in the day Flora passed through a pretty village. She slowed the car and looked up through the windshield at the gathering clouds of evening.

Hundreds of chimney swifts, chattering and twittering, found dinner in the evening air, last morsels before coming to fitful rest for the first and only time since morning. As they darted they argued among themselves, discussing their perch for the night. They searched, dived and dipped, formed a wide circle and began a black funnel downward only to change their minds and rise again on wicked batlike wings. They were seeking the best part of town, the finest, choicest section to dirty, as they rustled and bickered through the night, eager for dawn. Sooty, anxious insomniacs, nervous with energy, they were irritably ready to endure the night, get through it, in order to set out again and spend another day gouging deep lines in the pure blue sky.

HE moved his arm from around her waist to the middle of her back. With his other he gently collapsed the joint of her knee. She buckled and sank into his arms. He carried her to the bed. There he made handcuffs with his left hand, holding her ankles together so that her legs could not separate. With his right hand he began lightly to feather the hair of her mons, brushing over the sensitive bud with almost imperceptible strokes. Her gaze was focused at a distant point, but was attentive. The increasing size of her pupils caused ripples of darkness to grow over the deep blue of her eyes. After his fingers had played for a while she moved to spread her legs to receive his touches more fully, but he held her ankles tighter, gripped with the circles of his fingers, and rubbed, rubbed her, then ran his tongue along her thighs. She began to struggle, unconsciously, still in her concentration, as he held her legs, banded together, tight to the bed. She moved a bit from one side to the other, her arms beginning to push at his shoulders. She arched her back, trying for more feeling, deeper in, urging, encouraging his moves. Her eyes glazed and closed, she began to moan, plaintive, melancholy sobs of loss.

He didn't touch her breasts, had not attempted to kiss her. He had sat on the edge of the bed and taken her ankles in his hand. Now he knelt beside the bed and with his mouth did what his right hand had been doing. Feathered the bud with his tongue. He gauged her sobs and at length, suddenly, released his grip on her ankles. Her legs sprang apart, her knees locked rigid, her calves bunched, her toes in points. He plunged, at the same time, a finger into her rectum and his tongue into her wet opening. She cried out.

"I SWEAR," said Harley. "Look at this. This is the worst goddamn shower I ever been under. Look at the color of that water. Hardly even warm. Feels like some fool redneck is spitting tobacco juice on you. If it wasn't for the company I'd be outa here in two seconds. Uh-huh! Just look at those tits!" He moved his hands.

"Hell," said Harley. "You thought you were going to be a nurse? I wanted to be a goddamned engineer. TVA. I figured to be the best goddamned engineer in the whole fucking TVA. Take out a riverbed, throw in a coffer dam, put in them needle valves and cylinder gates, shut off that stream slick as a whistle. Oh,

Christ, I don't know. Here I am in that shit-eating town whoring wheels.

"Uhm!" he said. "That's nice. Here. Take hold of this. Hey now. I bleeve the boy's ready to go again."

Headlights of passing cars streaked across the walls and ceiling, flashes of illumination that flared, then dimmed, the whine of shifting gears from trucks meeting the challenge of the curve that lay a few yards beyond the window. Door slammings, shouts and greetings of salesmen, drummers, cries of, "Hey there, tootsie," or "Meet ya in five."

The sounds of flesh on flesh, shifting bodies, the slide of sheets over skin, rearrangements of weight on bedsprings, elbows, the fling of her loosened hair as she rose to sit astride him, the flat of his palm to her nipples.

"A pause," said Harley. He grasped her hips to stop her movement. "A pause for reflection. Goddamn, Flora. I want you to promise me we can get together back at home."

She looked at him, flat, distant.

"I swear to God I'll go limp if you say no."

"All right," said Flora. "Sure. All right, Harley. Why not? Why the hell not?"

"Well, okay, then, honey," he said, changing his position. "You've just bought your ticket. Coast to coast. I am now gonna fly you coast to coast, transcontinental, nonstop. No need to refuel *this* boy. All right, doll, are you ready for takeoff? Here we go. We're rising . . . we're in the air. This is historic, folks, you are witness to a historic flight . . . on the beam . . . we're on the beam . . . wait . . . there's some turbulence . . . we're encountering some turbulence . . ." he shouted, rollicking her breasts with his hands ". . . now lifting . . . lifting . . . this here is your pilot speee . . ."

At dawn Flora got into her car alone. As she drove away from the group of tourist cabins, she saw off to one side a flock of songbirds flying toward her, headed, she thought, for a meadow and pond on her left. She gathered speed as she watched them. One bird separated slightly from the group and flew closer to her car than the others—sailing, its wings outstretched, its eyes bright. The road curved toward it.

AFTER a while we didn't talk much. We went into the living room after dinner. He smoked and held the newspaper to keep him company. I stood at the window, my face pressed so close to the pane that cold and moisture fogged my vision. I saw the world through a vapor that alternately rose and diminished as I breathed and wept.

"She'll be back, you know," he said one evening.

"But she's gone away. With lots of bags." How could I convey to him the finality of her leave-taking? "She's driven away in her *car*," I tried.

"She drives the car," he said, "but night drives a woman. When it gets dark enough, black enough, she'll be back."

How could the darkness of one deep night be measured against any other? She had gone, and he had promised to die. I had heard him tell her over and over again that he promised to die.

"You go on to bed," he told me.

I had forgotten how to sleep. When I lay down my tongue grew in my mouth, pressed against my palate, pushed with monumental force against the teeth that trapped it.

When I elided into sleep I dreamed of a hideous, chattering monkey that I lusted to torment and kill, but it was so disgusting, so foul to me that my hands refused to touch it, even to close around its excrescence of a neck, and I woke in a sweat of revulsion. Hours passed. I heard the night birds go through their repertoire. The freight train hooted. The curtains stirred and the leaf patterns were skeletons. I got up to see if her car was in sight.

Maybe I was mistaken. Maybe it wasn't what I thought and she wanted to come home, was ready to come home, but was lost. It was just that she couldn't find her way.

She didn't know the prisoner-on-the-run thumbnail trick to find her direction, I was almost certain of that. Too bad, because the polish made her nail so shiny.

She could buy a compass, though. They had them in Woolworth's. Round metal case clasping the scratchy glass, ornate letters, N, S, E, W, then in between those sw, se, ne, nw, a circle of possible points. The face of the compass wore cabalistic designs and in the center of the device a needle lay bouncing on a tenuous mounting. I wasn't sure she knew how to use a compass. The theory had been explained to me several times but it made no sense at all. The needle was a fickle thing hurriedly waving its arms first one way, then summoning the traveler in another, enough to confuse a Leif Erikson.

I saw her standing outside Woolworth's in some quaint, distant village holding the compass in her cupped hand. I saw her purse tucked under her arm, the traveling suit she wore, the furrow on her brow as she tried to decipher the information compass offered. The irritated "Well, which way?" of her glance, and then I saw her reach the limit of her patience. She hurled the compass into the public trash basket. She returned to her car and sat drumming her fingers on the steering wheel.

She unfolded a map. She turned it on its side and then entirely upside down as she traced a line of its circulatory system with squinting intensity. I urged her on, sending mental reassurances, but she lost the thread in a snarl of capillaries. Fussed, she crumpled the map into a ball and threw it out the car window.

She could ask people directions, but they would be so charmed by her company they would try to detain her. Or maybe nobody would recognize the name of our town or know where it was. Or she might not happen to pick the right people to ask, the people who *did* know. She could spend years driving, retracing, floundering, at last even forgetting the question "How do I get home?" And then traveling, drifting to no purpose at all, a wanderer forever.

Or something might happen to her car, and she'd have to travel on foot. Like the Indians, creep into the forest, moccasins of doeskin, soft and silent, fringe of her suede dress moving ever so slightly. Follow the bend in the river, birdsong, deer path; track her way reading the winds, the stars; return to her own tribe, her campfire.

How could the stars lead someone home? The Big Dipper told me nothing. What did people mean when they said "Follow the stars"? It didn't seem logical. If you followed a star, you would go up into the air, into the sky, into the heavens.

She would soar above the treetops. She would skim past pine and spruce in the resinous air that green needles had embroidered into the atmosphere. Down the hazy blue sides of mountains, vapor clouds pillowing the stones and boulders to softness. She could see the intensity of rivers and streams, read the earth itself, then wheel and turn with joyous vigor at the articulation of wing in shoulder, and with the excited pull of tendon beat her wings, push herself homeward, soul bursting with delight.

I returned to bed. I lay there. I worried about my father's hands.

He, the person, was invincible. He was the definitive embodiment of an adult male: the general disposition toward brusqueness, that off-putting, haughty exclusiveness composed of whiskers, overcoats, and cigarette smoke. That whiff of outdoors and grand accomplishment that rides in on the hat brim. His identifying sound of keys and coins, those first cousins of the pocket, in league with men to open serious doors, make endless careless purchases. His scathing assessment of what he took as signs of weakness or the effete in other men—if they wore gloves in winter, say, or worse, carried an umbrella in anticipation of rain, or indeed walked under one if it came.

Because he scorned gloves, his hands, in harsh weather, became chapped, cracked, bruised. It was his only sign of vulnerability.

Could death enter through the hands? Could it come to settle in his cupped palm at night? As the covers rose and fell with his breathing—the sheet turned neatly down, his head tilted back, mouth silently open, his breathing steady—could the small black cat of death come creeping to nestle in his palm? Could it turn its triangular head and, with a brush of its whiskers across his thumb, sink needle teeth into the injuries of his hand and claim my father?

"What about our tramps through the woods?!" I wanted to sit up and cry out to him. "Our trips to the mill? The Sunday rides? Watch out!" I wanted to shriek.

Minnie was gone, Rawlings vacant. My mind closed when I tried to think of Randolf. My mother was cruising the land in her coupe, a fleeting shade, always in mind but never present. And soon my father would leave for some deep chill waters where the old browns and rainbows flicked their tails and ignored the bait for all eternity.

And I was a minnow, a scrap of a fingerling, jerked first one way and then another, left dangling and unclaimed on the thread of an abandoned line, wafted here and there but with the scar of the barbed hook embedded firmly and forever in my mouth. My portion.

SCHOOL began again. Sadie readied me in the mornings, Lily Mae walked me to dance class or to the homes of my friends.

My new teacher in school was a tall woman with red hair,

efficient, kind but brisk, an acute observer of her pupils. She detected a waning interest in my attentiveness and quickly called my father to inform him that I needed corrective lenses. He took me for glasses and my work improved.

I moved into my body, took possession of my childhood, reached out to children my age with a liveliness and alertness, a sense of belonging that I had never known.

I chanted to age-old singsongs of skip rope. I patted wet red earth over my balled fist and squatted patiently, waiting for the mud to recompose itself into dry clay, withdrew my hand with care, slowly, and there!—a toad house. I joined my classmates for Saturday serials at the moving-picture show and sat, popcorn suspended before my open mouth, and watched with approval as the secret door to the pyramid slid down the thieving intruder's back, sealing him forever into the pharaoh's tomb.

Hide-and-seek. Locate a nook, a cranny, squirm into it, body compacted and alert, then through chink or peephole spy on the hunter, and hold, with primeval instinctive knowledge, the breath. I discovered the complicity of the hunted, who by the very act of hiding, assume a guilt. And who then, to exculpate it, prickle—with the complicitor's stare—the nape of the hunter's neck. And as the hunter turns, the prey, in rapturous death-wish offer, sends out the silent cry "Look this way! Here I am!"

My father bought me a bicycle and strode along beside me in the early evenings, steadying the machine with one hand as I stood, knees trembling, calves knotted, pushing the pedals that rose and fell, completed their circles, from my energy and determination. Wind caught in my hair, my nose reddened in the late sun, a beading of sweat moistened my brow, my upper lip, my underarms. It was a heady freedom to pump and push and finally to pull away, leaving my father proud and smiling, standing on the sidewalk in his toga, he a Caesar, an Augustus, while I, the loyal legionnaire, rode off in my chariot, devoted, honorable, deserving of trust.

My sleep was sound. It was the sleep of oblivion, of exhaustion. I slept all night. I remembered no dreams, or if I did they were the minor visions of repeated daily acts: over and over I tied my shoes or gathered my school books or put clothing in dresser drawers.

Days of calm, days of containment. We were a family: a husband, a wife, a child. Our days followed one another in orderly fashion.

SHE came home in the middle of the night.

I can't say how long she was gone. I do remember, though, before her return, Trudy and another of Flora's bridge-club friends stopped by the house. They said that Dot was back in town and—they directed their questions to Sadie—they were just curious to know if Mr. Simpson had shared with the help the expected date of his wife's arrival. Understand, they just needed to know in order to get up their foursomes, they were not prying. For all her irritation toward Flora in person, Sadie in this case came down squarely on the side of family loyalty and routed the women with a shuffling display of feigned incomprehension.

It was late one night, almost at dawn, when I heard the front door open. He was sitting in the living room, waiting. It may be that he had gotten a phone call during the day, I don't know.

I ran to the head of the stairs. She stood in the hall covered with diamonds, with rain, with glass.

"I hit a bird," she said. "It broke the windshield and came through the glass. It died as it hit my face."

"Oh my God," said my father.

"But it didn't hurt me," she said in wonderment. "It hit my face softly. It brushed my face softly with its feathers. I felt its beak and its thin wire feet touched me"—she removed an invisible cobweb from her cheek—"but it didn't hurt me at all."

He put his arm around her and led her up the stairs. They passed me on the landing.

"It didn't know the road would curve," she said. "It was flying in a line. How could it know, how could a bird know, that the road would curve?"

He put her to bed and sat beside her, holding her hand, stroking her arm as if to mend it. Flora wept.

EIGHT

My mother read. She lost interest in cards, refused to go to the moving-picture shows, on shopping trips. For a while Sadie answered incessant daytime phone calls from Harley that came while my father was at work. Flora didn't take them. She sat during the day in a rocker, so unlike her that I was often startled, as I returned from play, to see a woman on the porch, near the ferns and ivy—a strange, still woman sitting on our porch turning the pages of a book.

By late autumn she seemed more herself. They talked, my parents. They conversed, they told each other things. They looked at each other. He paused to hold her hand in his before he left the house.

They made plans of a vague sort—trips to the mountains, improvements on the house—discussed the town and how it was growing, talked of the books she read, had dinner with new friends. A placid but rich life between them.

A quiet Christmas passed.

February came again, and on the way home from school I threw all my valentines down the storm sewer.

That summer they spent together. They went to the lake and he taught her to fish, she gamely and awkwardly cast, her elbow making an angular, tentative geometry of a movement that he performed with ease and grace. Their heads bent together as they baited hooks, stood, the waters lapping at their feet, the waves gently returning and returning to the shore where the two stood in sunlight, in harmony, I thought in love. They went out in the rowboat. I saw their figures move between the pilings of the bridge and then, smaller and smaller, disappear downstream, water sparkling, voices laughing, arms waving, as I stood on shore, held by Gabe's hand, told that I was a fisherman, too, but that he and I would stay on land, we would wait on shore by the edge of the lake for the afternoon to wane, grow mellow, for the light to turn hazy. Then the air freshened and the boat returned.

FOREIGNERS invaded. They used force on the hands of the typesetter for the local newspaper. They compelled him to print the preposterous names of *their* generals and *their* cities on *our* front page. They burst into the projection booth of the movie house, strong-armed Johnny Weissmuller aside and then *they* swung out over our heads, leaped to giant size, and landed with their tall, tight boots pounding on the stage of the Carolina. They stole our sugar and our meat and our shoe leather and caused our government to give us instead booklets of ration stamps. Every citizen, even children, received such a book. My number was 526610.

READ BEFORE SIGNING

In accepting this book, I recognize that it remains the property of the United States Government. I will use it only in the manner and for the purposes authorized by the Office of Price Administration. *Void if altered.*

The black stamps were marked "spare" and had no illustration. The blue stamps, above the heavy block letter and number, bore a head of ripened wheat; the red, a horn of plenty; the green, the hand and torch of the Statue of Liberty—the new heroine, along with Betty Grable, of the nation.

Each time Flora tore stamps out of my book my heart sank. If the stamps were removed, the book was *altered*. I couldn't seem to get this point across to her. Finally she grew so exasperated with my nattering that I desisted and silently submitted to the inevitability of federal prison. I chose my favored possessions and packed them, ready to depart, practiced combing my hair with my wrists clamped together, brushing my teeth in such manner as well.

From an ordered world which had bedrooms and bacon and a proper number of bureau drawers for its inhabitants, the whole planet changed in a matter of months to a place where people vied for hotel rooms or slept in barracks with their belongings crammed into metal lockers at their feet.

Travel became chancy. The armed forces had "priority" and private citizens were often "bumped" from trains and buses, so that troops could be transferred, or a single soldier go home on leave to say good-bye to his mother. The "bumped" person speculated for weeks on the event, guessing which invasion he had, actually, in a way really, participated in bringing off. Gasoline was rationed, too, and Flora gave many of her coupons to my father since she stayed home so much. Miss Elsie was designated air-raid warden at the mill and staged surprise drills, which were no surprise because she invariably held them during lunch hour to save working time for the war effort. She coveted one of the big "E for Effort" flags for the factory.

"First," said Randolf, one of our boys in blue, "they take carbon dioxide, a gas, and compress it into a liquid. Actually change the physical form of it," he explained directly to me, "from something you *can't* see into something you *can* see. This liquid is then cooled until it becomes a kind of snow. That's three states," he addressed everyone else. "Gas to liquid to solid. Then this snow is taken, and under terrible pressure, intense pressure"–he began to move his outstretched hands closer and closer together, the arms trembling, corded with the effort—"under terrible pressure" —and he looked at her, engaging her, mesmerizing her—"they WHOMP!" he shouted, and clapped his hands together, to make the sound of a huge machine clanging shut, so that Adelaide shrieked and jumped. "There you are," he smiled. "Dry ice."

We stood in the kitchen while Randolf explained one of the aspects of his service expertise, a new field for him. "Stores." He slit open with a knife one side of the heavy-padded brown paper envelope he had brought with him. He inserted the knife and withdrew on its blade some lumps of dead gray matter. White smoke rose to drift and scud around his face and shoulders. I reached out the tip of a finger to touch the stuff.

"No!" He spoke loudly, and grasped my wrist. "Don't touch it! It burns."

"Ah. Of course," said my father.

"When a substance is icy enough, cold enough, it burns," said Randolf. "Its chill is perceived by human touch as heat." The gray bits sat smoldering on the kitchen counter.

"And it's poison," he told us. "Not like lye or strychnine, but it will kill you just the same. If ingested, it freezes the windpipe. It freezes flesh but"—he paused—"it boils water."

He placed the stopper in the kitchen sink and drew several inches of water. Taking a scrap of the brown paper he lifted chunks of the ice and laid them on the surface. They sank. The clear water turned gray and frothed into a nasty, foaming mass. A nest of vipers roiled, tangled, then grew quiet.

"It melted," I said.

"Actually, it doesn't melt," said Randolf. He indicated the bits still fogging and misting on the counter. They had grown smaller, but there was no water to be seen circling their base. "It sublimes," he said.

"What?" asked Flora. "What does it do?"

"It doesn't melt, it sublimes," he said. "But even that, slowly. It keeps for days. And another thing," he continued, extricating me from the edge of the counter where I hung suspended on my folded arms, legs dangling, "don't put your nose over it. There must be a proper source of fresh air at all times or the carbon dioxide tends to replace oxygen in the lungs."

As we waited in the vestibule Adelaide's face grew flushed: a holly berry surrounded by mistletoe. I was delirous with the romance of the occasion. I wore a long pink dress, pink slippers. Randolf was wearing his uniform. Flora, for once, made no fuss over her own dress, choosing something almost at the last minute from her closet, but silently helped me with mine. Adelaide, wonderful Adelaide, bestowed on me an honor and importance far surpassing even my wildest yearnings. I stood at the head of the aisle, the white aisle-cloth stretched for miles before me, flowers and holly and evergreens in loops and wreaths, velvet ribbons. Faces turned, expectant, excited. The music heightened. I was handed a white satin cushion and on it, couched in a satin crush so that they would not slip in my nervous grasp, were two gold hoops. The cushion, trimmed with lace, I carried on my hands, stretched out before me, down the aisle, past the guests. All faces turned to me, as though I were responsible for bringing about the union we were gathered to celebrate. Even the two tiny round faces, the circles on the pillow, looked up at me, seeming to smile. All the faces in the church turned to look as I bore down the aisle the twin wedding rings, the bedded pair.

WARTIME considerations dictated many of the wedding decisions. Randolf was stationed closer to our town than to Adelaide's, so her family consented to the couple's earnest request to have the wedding at our church and in our town instead of theirs. This way the newlyweds could have more time together before Randolf was shipped overseas. The reception was at our house instead of out at the country club, to save the guests gasoline. And as the centerpiece of the table, instead of a sugarless wedding cake, two turtledoves billed and cooed, their heads tilted so that the soft, downy neck-hollow of each presented itself to the other—vulnerable, throbbing, touching in love and trust. A clear sparkling couple carved of ice.

After the wedding we all went back—all the wedding party, guests, relatives—to the stone house for the reception. People sat everywhere, at the table in the dining room, in the living room, on the stairs in the front hall. Crowds of people. Women in laces and sashes and low necklines wore slippery-soled new shoes for which they had surrendered ration coupons. Men, their faces shined, suits pressed, wore heavy silk ties. Some uniforms, many sparkling jewels. Laughing, celebrating, drinking, joking.

And after the party when everyone went home, after the tables were cleared and Sadie and Lily Mae and the others left, after the ice carving was placed in the old refrigerator with its laboring coils on top and packed in dry ice for long keeping, after Flora had the very special pleasure of introducing Adelaide to the whole town, after the married couple went down the hall to Randolf's room where my father insisted they stay when no hotel could be booked, after all these things, then, as a very special gift "to the new couple" from Dot and Harley, then, we heard, Flora heard, far into the night, from the church tower, the vestrymen playing the chimes. As Flora lay down the hall from Randolf once more, a malicious and reunited Dot and Harley caused to be rung over and over the sweet, the lovely sweet bells. The whole town listened, and laughed at Flora, as they heard ringing, far into the wedding night, the beautiful, the golden sweet sound of the wedding chimes.

WE stood beside my mother's bed looking down at her. She was still breathing but in a dragging shallow way. Her face was sallow and her lips parted. Though she was still alive, she had left the living world behind.

"NOT pneumonia," the doctor had said when he first called on her, "or TB. It's a chill. A prolonged, persistent, unyielding chill. Causing congestion."

It had come to settle in her chest, clung there, a stubborn homesteader, not to be dislodged in spite of incursions of tawny spiced tea and spoonings of syrups in various barbaric colors.

A rubber hot water bottle, raw, trembling, attached its febrile body to hers. Some inner organ, it looked, come to the outside of her, rising and falling with her breath.

Dazzling white cloths were brought to her, folded, dipped into steaming mustard water, then wrapped in dry outer bandages—sharp packets of heat. Steam rose to flush her face.

She endured for a time the ministrations of Sadie, allowing her to replenish the hot packs, the boiling water, but soon grew better and insisted on going to the kitchen herself to make her own packs. I heard pots clanging, the stove flared on and off, the refrigerator door opened as she checked the turtledoves packed in their dry ice–conscientious, ready to alert my father, ill as she was, if more dry ice were needed.

She became ill only days after the wedding. Along with her illness, seeming to be part of it, she became compulsive about maintaining the ice carving of the tutledoves, opening the refrigerator time after time to check on them. Then she became embarrassed about the compulsion, didn't want us to observe it, sent me out of the kitchen to fetch more cloth to wind around her hot packs, dispatched Sadie, saying she thought the telephone had rung. She implored my father to order more dry ice, and then more again, to pack around the pair of birds.

I often sat by her bed reading to her from my geography book; she said that was her favorite subject. I read to her about people who rode on the humped, hairy backs of camels, of Central America, where great flights of amber stairs were stained brown by the blood of the sacrificed, of the tulips that waved to the passing Zuider Zee–that body of water delinquent of banks, held at bay by a boy's fingertip. She watched my face more than listened to the words. Once she reached her hand out from under the covers and took my hand. Although I saw wisps of fog rising from the pack clutched tightly to her chest, her touch chilled me to the bone, and her lips were blue.

"I don't know what to say," she said, and tears came into her eyes.

YESTERDAY, or the day before, I didn't remember which, they had removed from her swelling wrist her tiny silver watch. As her illness progressed she had glanced at it more and more frequently, stabbing my heart deeper every time. Then my father gave her his pocket watch, unclasping it from the chain and laying it on the pillow beside her face. He meant it as an act of solace, of comfort, but she looked at his watch with a bitter smile of memory or recognition, as if it had somehow once betrayed her. Then she closed her eyes and turned her head away.

"Edema has set in," the doctor now told us.

"What does that mean, edema?" asked my father.

The doctor turned back the covers. In a disturbing gesture of almost sexual ownership, he slid my mother's gown up her legs to the knees, revealing her once slender ankles and calves. He made a bracelet of his thumb and forefinger and banded her ankle. He pressed. When he withdrew his hand the imprint from his thumb remained behind as a dent in her pale, waterlogged flesh.

She had had few visitors. She saw Trudy and Winnie, but Dot never called, certainly not Harley. Tansy's mother was gone, having made her ultimate choice between sleep and waking. Randolf and Adelaide visited while he was on leave, her waist already thickening, her stomach just beginning to push against her dress. Flora seemed glad to see them, asked them to come again soon, her manner no different with them than with any other visitors.

Her sisters had come to nurse her, sitting one at a time in shifts by her bed—sitting beside her with their familial variations of the face that lay, open-mouthed, on the pillow. In a startling double way, Flora both lay and sat, both suffered and consoled, held her own hand, smoothed her own brow. She both endured and ended.

Toward the end when she remembered anything, Flora remembered a smiling blue-eyed man, leather reins slung around his neck, mule and plow leading him across an endless open field of empty earth. Through the years of her life, through time, she had almost forgotten who she was back then, or what it was that the child, Flora, had really wanted when the primitive male call rose from her father's lips, "Whooo? Whooo?" and the resounding answer he gave himself, "Minnie! Minnie! My Min!" The child, Flora, had heard a love song, a crying of love so fierce that the name of the beloved, called out, took to the sky, circled the globe, and returned from all the universe to claim its owner.

THAT night I walked to the row of windows in my room and looked out. I stood in the dark, in my gown, and felt the dampness of air that carried both the chill and softness of spring. I stared at the silver night-shine on the road out of town. I sat for a while on the window ledge. From time to time a car passed, tires making the lonely sound of midnight travel. A night bird was crying.

I never saw the bird. That other bird, the one that died to send her home. I saw the shattered windshield. I saw the shards of glass in her car, in her hair, glistening on her face, chips of glass falling from her clothes. But I never saw any feathers or any blood or the slightest of marks on her lovely face. I never saw the bird.

But as she lay dying I did see the scars, the burns. Deep and terrible and scarlet. The burns that I gave her, the scars that I gave her when I delivered Randolf's valentine—when I inflicted on her, on Flora, on my mother, the most terrible torment the world has ever known. False hope. And when she held the ice to her chest, when she wrapped into the cloth packs not heat but cold, she only did it to stop the pain. I saw the scars. I saw the burns that froze her heart to death.

As the breeze shifted on the still-contained buds of the trees, a beam of moonlight revealed the hook-and-eye latch of the screen. I undid the hook. I undid the hook for me, the helpless infant who had been latched into the covered crib so often. Then I nudged the screen so that it fell with a soft thud to the ground below.

I grasped the window frame and swung my legs over the sill. They dangled against the cold outside wall of the house; my gown floated like a mist around my ankles.

I leaned out, away from the house, far out into the night,

and threw my arms around the slender, powdered white body of the birch tree. I clung to its trunk, my heart pounding, my cheek pressed against its curling leather bark. I peered up through its branches to the moon, the planets, the stretches of visible sky.

After a while I climbed down from the tree and moved out into the moonlight, I left the stone house, and I left a sleeping man whose wife had once, long ago, almost come to love him.

That night, I began to wander. I became a child who wandered, who roamed, at night. I began my first trip, the first of my secret, nighttime journeys. They were trips into the dark, out of the town, trips on the night-shining road. They were trips that I took for my mother, for Flora, in case not even God could bring her peace.